Black Hills Gold

Black Hills Gold

A Novel

Scott Thomas Young

ISBN: 0692608931
ISBN 13: 9780692608937
Library of Congress Control Number: 2015921494
Gigigabi Books: Wilmette, IL

IF NOT FOR his love of books, Brave Eagle would certainly not be alive. As a contingent split off the reservation towards Wounded Knee, he saw the move as timely opportunity to leave the tribe. It was not so much he did not agree with the Ghost Dancers. After all, the dancers wished Jesus or another messiah would come and save the red man and wipe out the white man, and Brave Eagles' father was a white man.

Betty Pettigrew, the librarian had offered him a job many times and he thought the time had come. He told his wife, Shaded Feather, the mission of his journey was to get more books, but he had a different destiny in mind.

Brave Eagle carried himself well for a fifty-year-old brave. He was six-feet tall, lean and lithe, with hard cut arms and firm legs. Only his hair betrayed that he was of mixed heritage: it curled in its length, unlike the straight black manes of his fellow braves. His face was sun drenched and a line creased his forehead. He was a man who liked to laugh, but laughter evaded him. Joy was in the past. Long past.

In the tribe, he was respected as a heroic warrior who feared no one and emerged from battles unscathed and unwounded, almost like he was protected. It put him in a category with Crazy Horse, but there was that one big issue. Brave Eagle never sought glory and recognition. That was for Crazy Horse, who claimed he killed Custer, but it had actually been Brave Eagle who fired the fatal shot. Crazy Horse shot an already dying man.

He barely set foot inside the tiny library entrance, when Betty Pettigrew, a diminutive firebrand of a librarian, silver haired but strikingly pretty fifty one year old, gaped in astonishment.

"You are alive!"

The library consisted of three rooms. It was a converted house and Betty Pettigrew designated a fiction room, a non-fiction room and a children's room. In the entrance way, stood her desk and a long table. She put her hand on his shoulder as if to steady him for the news.

Brave Eagle shrugged, "Of course I am. It may have been a couple of months since you last saw me, but I did not age that much!"

He dropped the canvas satchel he used to carry books to a table and brushed the dust from his trousers. "Any new books?"

"You don't know what happened at Wounded Knee?"

"No." The utter horror in her voice betrayed that it was very bad.

"Many were killed. Let me get the newspaper."

She retrieved a newspaper from behind her desk and gave it to Brave Eagle, who pulled a chair and read. It took two minutes to absorb the newspaper article, and then he put it down, and read it a second time.

"It does say some survived." A pale emptiness filled his gut. He leaned his elbows on the table and held his face in his fists.

"Maybe she is alive."

"Maybe." Betty referred to Shaded Feather, his wife, but he had no doubt she was dead. But what of Onashola?

"I will go back."

"You should probably wait until morning. There is a storm coming. Stay in the little house tonight."

The long, slow journey by carriage was made difficult by numerous stops to make the road through new snow passable. At one point, Brave Eagle spent four hours digging blown snow away from the road. But, as Betty put it, "he was alive," and if not for the sojourn to the library, that may have been his fate. From the library, he brought his favorite book, Robinson Crusoe. Betty told him it was written about a real man, not an imaginary story. Crusoe was like him, a man nothing could kill. His father, now long deceased, owned one book, the Holy Bible, and on his visits to the reservation, he told Brave Eagle of the stories within that book and made his son want to learn to read. From a missionary woman, he learned the basics of reading, and from there, he taught himself.

He had left Shaded Feather behind at Wounded Knee. There was almost no need to see the list of names. He knew. She had found her place with all the others, in a mass grave.

He expected Shaded Feather might have run straight at the soldiers and asked them to shoot her. She lived with blackness all around her. The source of despair was the Battle against the Golden haired warrior, Custer, at Little Big Horn. Yes, that was a decisive victory for the Sioux, but they had losses, too, and among them were Shaded Feather's two sons, Two Tomahawks and Slight Arrow. After their deaths, his wife retreated into some other world and Brave Eagle learned his existence no longer mattered to her.

She was barren with Brave Eagle and his choices led to this, no possessions, a handful of books, a horse, a carriage and Bone, his scruffy black-and-white spotted three-legged dog. What should he do?

From the news accounts, an Indian fired at the soldiers first, and provoked a volley of shots and a rout. Women and children were killed. The soldiers went crazy. If he discovered the man who took Shaded Feather's life, he would hunt and kill him. But systematically seeking revenge, one at a time, he might have done at twenty, but now he was fifty, and what did it matter? He had nothing. He survived the wars unscathed. He could go into the thickness of battle and come out without a scratch. Brave Eagle wondered if God wanted him to live, for what reason.

When he took Shaded Feather as his wife, she was a widow with two teenaged boys. Many times, he pondered how to please her, but she always lived under a black cloud. "I don't want to live," she said more than once, even before Little Big Horn. He could have chosen another woman, but he picked the one who wanted to die. He might have walked over to another teepee and declared a divorce.

He rode out to Wounded Knee, where it all happened. After the battle at Wounded Knee, a blizzard covered the ground and for two days the bodies lay strewn across the field, in the ravines, frozen in death. Some survived the onslaught of rifles only to freeze to death in the cold, and for those that did survive, many suffered from severe frostbite. Brave Eagle thought the first impulse, when confronted with so many soldiers, would be to run for the ravine and protection. He did not believe the myth that the Ghost Dance cloak gave one invincibility from bullets. In fact, he did not believe a lot about his tribe's myths, as he did not totally accept the myths in the Bible. Moses parting the sea?

The wind whipped across the plains and he covered his mouth with a wool scarf and the pellets stung his eyes. He wore a wide-brimmed hat with a round crown and a fur coat reached his ankles. He was aware some-where beneath his feet lay Shaded Feather. The wind whistled, almost screaming, echoing the voices of those below. The white earth with an inch of frozen snow covered an open prairie of shrub grass. Bone whimpered and sniffed the ground. Perhaps the dog smelled the cadavers, or at least sensed them. Across the field, two white men, a photographer and his assistant, took pictures.

The burnt-out wooden frames of teepees clung precariously to the earth as the wind gusts threatened to topple them. Brave Eagle's possessions were all in the carriage- a case of clothes, books, and relics. As the soldiers searched the teepees, he wondered what one would have thought if they found a copy of David Copperfield. Again, he doubted the soldiers would know Dickens from Shakespeare, if they read at all.

She was now, finally at peace. Brave Eagle crossed himself, involuntarily, and realized the irony. He was a Catholic, converted by a Priest. But many in his tribe took the message and after witnessing the greed and lust of the white man to take all the land, that God had to be just, and the idea spread that Jesus would come back and justice would prevail. Yet, he asked, Jesus too was a white man, killed by other white men. And red men fought and killed other red men, so who said there was a chosen people? The white men who slaughtered his people alleged to be Christians and fighting for the glory of God.

Dust, to dust they say. Shaded Feather's depression hung over Brave Eagle so much he read and retreated into a world of stories. He hoped for her sake, death had been painless.

"Father, I don't want to sleep any more," she said in her sleep once. Undoubtedly, her brother, Yellow Breast died at Wounded Knee, one of the biggest believers in the Ghost Dance. But on the trip to the library, he had made a big decision. He would leave his tribe and live in Rapid City. Betty Pettigrew offered a job at the library, and a place to live. He planned only a return trip to give his wife an ultimatum, come with me to Rapid City or stay here. Instead, his return trip was to her grave.

He walked to the photographer, Bone sidling along with him. The man shuffled some metal plates and appeared to conclude his day of photography as the sun had little time left in the day.

"Were you here?" Brave Eagle asked.

"I was," the man said. "And you?"

"No, I am Lakota, but I was away."

"And lucky for you," the photographer said. His words froze in a puff of steam as they came out of his mouth Happened fast."

"Is the newspaper true? " Brave Eagle asked.

"One of the Indians shot and both the soldiers and the Indians started shooting, only a few feet from each other, twenty or thirty killed in seconds. The Indians ran, shooting back and looking for cover, and the soldiers chased them. Why they shot women and children, I don't know. Joseph and I ran to our wagon and stayed. The soldiers yelled out, "Remember Custer!" and kept shooting. They shot some who tried to surrender. I couldn't look."

Brave Eagle glanced around. How he could have survived the fight? Two hundred yards away was a forested area that offered shelter. He would have climbed a tree or dug himself into a bush. Brave Eagle did not come out of so many of Crazy Horse's battles without keeping his wits. There was a time to flee. Many a time, a young brave was killed in a foolhardy rush at the enemy, trying to prove his fiercely courageousness, stopped by a bullet to the brain that cared little about courage.

Whatever, the ghost dance was no more. Promises of invincibility proved unfounded. What a way to find out.

The ground was picked clean of any evidence a slaughter took place at such a barren spot, little protection from the merciless wind that slapped loose snow across his face. Once, the tribe chose where they lived and it was always a place of beauty and plenty, near streams and the buffalo. The white man came in, deciding they owned everything and the red man placed in the reservation. A man with a ledger book decided what plot was owned by whom and gave the Indians the worst land. Give them the Badlands. We don't want to live there.

Brave Eagle's little spot was destined to be a small wooden frame house next door to Mrs. Pettigrew in Rapid City and that would be a real change. Four walls and a stove, a bed and a table, two chairs and much more space than a teepee.

"Hey, Thomas, let's get one picture of this man with the three-legged dog before we leave. There's still enough light!" Joseph said.

"Can we?" Thomas, the photographer, asked. Brave Eagle shrugged. Maybe this would be in a newspaper.

"Fine. Don't print I am a survivor of Wounded Knee."

Brave Eagle lowered his scarf, held Bone by the ear and motioned for Bone to sit and face the camera. He glared into the lens and tried to express "Look what you have done. Are you happy now?' all in one photograph. When the light flashed and popped, he blinked and almost lost his balance. "Didn't mean to scare ya." Joseph laughed.

"You did not scare me," Brave Eagle smirked.

"I ask you, you're an Indian. So we got revenge for Custer. Do you think there will be revenge for this? If I were an Indian, I'd be on the warpath right soon."

"There is no one left to go on the warpath."

'Yeah. Guess not. But there are many other tribes. Comanches. Apaches. Will they seek revenge?"

Brave Eagle only snorted and walked away.

He left the massacre site for the Pine Ridge Reservation, in hopes of finding Onashola. He was directed to a list of survivors and inquired of her whereabouts. The list of the dead included almost everyone except for her. His wife, her brother, Onashola's family. He learned she was cared for in an Episcopal Mission. Four adult men survived the fight, and he sought out an old friend, Kicking Bear.

Kicking Bear was an elder man who dearly wanted the Ghost Dance to work magic, Brave Eagle found him on a cot in a one-bedroom house. A white swath of bandages covered his shoulders and taped one arm to his chest.

"Ah, the search for books saved you," Kicking Bear smiled.

"And what saved you?" Brave Eagle sat in a rocking chair across from the cot. Bone stayed outside and found a warmer spot beneath the front porch.

"We gave them our rifles and I needed to piss. So, I went off to the side and then a shot. It was the deaf Warrior Bob and an accident, but the soldiers opened fire. They killed thirty of us with the first shot, and I ran for the ravine. I stopped to fire and they shot me twice, in the face and shoulder, and I saw the soldiers kill the braves and chase the women and children.

I ran for the ravine and Onashola ran past me, with her baby on her back, she went down, struck by a bullet. I stopped for her, the baby was already dead but she did not know, and she got shot in the arm. We ran for the back of the ravine. She ran so much faster than me, she disappeared, until I heard her wailing and I climbed up behind some rocks where the baby lied out on the ground and she lay there and I put my hand over her mouth at first. I pulled her behind a boulder while the soldiers shot women and children.

We stayed all day and it grew cold and we found two children and their mother who played dead and protected themselves from the cold by stacking several bodies.

The blizzard came. A white storm, we could not see five paces from our eyes. Onashola would not let go of her dead baby. She whimpered and saying, "Little One."

We stayed in the same place for a day, the storm calmed down, but it froze and we heard voices. Come on, I said, we will die here. If they shoot us, we are dead anyway. So, Onashola, the woman and her two children came out and a few soldiers scanned the area, looking for survivors. But these men gave us blankets, hot drink and took us back here. Those that lived either pretended to be dead, or fell unconscious and managed to hide in the trees and bushes. Two women ran for a day only to freeze to death. White Lance, Joseph Horn Cloud, and Dewey Beard made it out alive. They were the only other men, besides me. Black Elk came up when it was almost over, and scared some soldiers away from killing the wounded."

Brave Eagle sat pensively, resting his hand on his face.

"Shaded Feather was in the first group killed. Her brother, and Flat Iron, too. They killed Big Foot; he was sick with pneumonia and tried to run. His body appeared in the newspaper, frozen stiff. This is the end, Brave Eagle. Sitting Bull warned us, they will keep coming and coming and overtake us and now we have no buffalo, only land that cannot grow a potato."

The ghost dance started the year before, when Wovoka, a member of the Peyote tribe in Nevada had a vision the night of a solar eclipse. As the moon covered the sun, he envisioned the day the Messiah would return and rid the earth of the white man. He danced, lifting one foot, dancing on the other and howling. He called his dance the Ghost Dance and he prescribed this dance as the magic that would hasten the Messiah's return.

Word spread to the tribes of the west, and some reported sightings of the Messiah, so the dance grew in fervor to the point the whites became alarmed and ordered the end of the dancing. It only made sense to ask them to stop dancing when the hoped-for result was the end of the white race.

Brave Eagle participated in a delegation of a dozen Lakota who trekked to Nevada to meet with Wovoka, and learn the dance. He was the only one skeptical of Wovoka's message; then again, he was the only one with white blood.

He pointed out, "Jesus was a white man, too."

"This might not be the same Jesus. This is a red Jesus, the brother of Jesus."

The theories kept shifting. Brave Eagle wanted to believe in the arrival of the Messiah, the answer was harmony among races, not the disappearance. And perhaps justice, getting rid of stupid rights and laws the white man made up as he went along.

The Lakota lived in desperate times, almost starving, their rations continuing to be cut, the government insisting they survive as farmers. No wonder they would look for a miracle.

Brave Eagle danced the Ghost Dance, despite his doubts. And when he danced, he felt a sense of freedom, like the sun surrounded his soul. He returned to his teepee after a night of dancing, excited, only to be greeted by his glum wife.

"For nothing," she sighed.

"You are right, but we need hope."

"Why? It makes it worse."

There was no arguing with her. Nothing made her optimistic. And when three hundred of the tribe left Pine Ridge for the creek where the man wounded in his knee was buried, Brave Eagle decided he wanted some more books. He had his vision quest early in his manhood, but this horse carriage ride with Bone proved to be of equal importance, for on this journey, he decided to leave the tribe completely.

Now, as he ventured to the Episcopal mission, Bone comfortable in the rear of the carriage, it took a glance at the empty seat beside him. That was where Shaded Feather sat silently, stone-faced. He loved her once, when she had life. Tears filled Brave Eagle's eyes and his body shook. The poor woman whose love for her sons was so strong that when they died, she did, too. The many friends lost their lives in a last-ditch dance for a better future, and the desperate state the massacre left the Lakota. The soldiers certainly wreaked their revenge over Custer, decimating an entire way of life. Brave Eagle only found retreat in books written by white men and women. That seemed to be a better place than the real world, inside those pages, where Robinson Crusoe survived his shipwreck and met his good man Friday. Brave Eagle felt alone on an island.

Onashola was one of about fifty that survived Wounded Knee. She was an extraordinary young woman Brave Eagle watched grow up on the reservation. In her childhood, she was the fleetest of youths and bested all the boys with the bow and arrow. He felt a kinship with the girl because, like him, she was a half-breed and that meant she had to be better than everybody else, overcoming the insults muttered against her and her mother. It was as likely Onashola survived, as it was Shaded Feather died, for one was a survivor and the other the living dead. Onashola's husband, Flat Iron, and her child, Little One, a six-month old boy died. Onashola was alone and Brave Eagle would find her.

What could he say to bolster the spirits of Onashola? Would she be like Shaded Feather and assume her life as over? She was the happiest and brightest of children growing up, embarrassing the boys with her athletic skills. She took up with one of the young Ghost Dancers, Flat Iron, and a brave with a hot temperament. It was doubtful Brave Eagle would approve of any who sought to marry Onashola. In his eyes, only a Chief was worthy of her. She would be starting over, too, as her entire family had been wiped out. She didn't even have a dog left.

He found her in a hastily assembled infirmary at the mission. As far as Brave Eagle knew, the only difference between the Catholics and the Episcopalians was the Pope was the Big Chief for the Catholics, and somebody in England ruled the Episcopalians.

He found her sitting in a chair, in a room with eight cots, six of them occupied with patients, the wounded from Wounded Knee. Onashola sat next to a cot with new linen, her arm bandaged and in a sling. She wore a shapeless poplin gown and moccasins. Her long, lustrous black hair was braided, and at the sight of Brave Eagle, she smiled, rose from her chair and embraced him with force.

When they broke their embrace, she wiped tears from her eyes.

"It is a joy to see you," Brave Eagle said.

"And for me to see you, Brave Eagle."

"And I am sorry about Little One, and your family."

With this, she started to cry, and Brave Eagle held her again, patting her back for a good five minutes before she composed herself.

"Onashola, I am moving to Rapid City. Will you come with me?"

She sniffled, "What's in Rapid City?"

"A woman offered work and a house to live in. "

"There is nowhere else to go." She agreed.

Onashola's belongings consisted of a pillow, a blanket, and an empty papoose. They left after she gave thanks to the mission Priest. She sat next to Brave Eagle, where Shaded Feather used to sit, and it gave Brave Eagle a lift. He had company in loss.

Surprisingly, Onashola talked on the ride to Rapid City, and told of how she survived the snowstorm beneath the dead. She remembered all the times Brave Eagle ran with her around the reservation. He taught her how to fish with a spear. He was a friend to her father, but she considered him her favorite of all the adults. She knew she disappointed him when she married Flat Iron, who Brave Eagle once called, Squatting Turd, But the eligible men were few, and she was twenty, so it was time.

She could not bring up her baby and finish a sentence before the tears overwhelmed her, and Brave Eagle put his arm on her shoulders as she cried.

"Why was I there?"

They arrived at the Rapid City library in mid-day of a frosty January morning, the ground frozen. Despite the cold, Bone jumped out of the carriage to wait at the front door for his master. Bone was a scruffy mongrel. Several years before, Brave Eagle spotted the mutt slinking around the library, limping. Brave Eagle looked in the dog's eyes and the dog communicated a need for help and lifted a mangled paw. He was a mixed breed, part German shepherd, part something else, and one glance at his shattered front left paw made Brave Eagle cringe. He sat on the ground, in the shrub grass, down the road from the library and petted the dog's head.

Brave Eagle took some whiskey from his satchel inside the carriage and walked slowly as the sixty-pound shepherd struggled with every step. Bone had not eaten in a week. Brave Eagle poured a cup of whisky and let Bone lap it up and he waited for Bone to fall asleep. When the dog finally slept, Brave Eagle straddled him, took his right leg and with the blade of his Bowie knife, sawed through at the dog's knee. The dog squirmed, yipping, and Brave Eagle sat hard upon him, wincing as the dog howled in pain, and with one hard thrust, held the dog's severed lower leg in his hand and Bone collapsed, unconscious.

Brave Eagle wrapped the stump that remained in a shirt, tied it tight. From that day, he had a three-legged dog that loved him. Bone's favorite resting spot was in the shade of the front porch of a tree outside the library, and he curled into a ball to rest. He stood this kind of chill without protection during the day but most winter nights found him nestled in the crawl space below the house next to Betty Pettigrew's. Before Brave Eagle, he had survived in much more primitive conditions, a miner's dog in camps near creek beds frequented by coyotes. The miner died in his boots one day, the victim of overexertion, a seventy year old man swinging a pick axe all day, searching for that strike that he could bring home to St. Louis. Bone stayed by that man's side for a week, keeping buzzards away, when he followed a horse-drawn cart that led him to Rapid City and shortly after, Brave Eagle.

His hair was so matted; Brave Eagle had borrowed Betty's hairbrush and painstakingly undid the mats, uncovering other wounds and scars. Whatever Bone had experienced, Brave Eagle did not know, but he was sure this dog had the will to live, much like himself.

Brave Eagle escorted Onashola inside. The library was set originally a three-room schoolhouse, organized as fiction, non-fiction, and children's books. Mrs. Pettigrew arranged the non-fiction books according to the Dewey decimal System, a new method of classifying books. She had worked in the University library as a student.

"Welcome back. And who is this?" She nodded to Onashola.

"Onashola."

"Shaded Feather?"

"Dead."

"I'm so sorry." She put her hand on Brave Eagle's forearm. He touched her hand and she let go.

"Onashola lost her husband, brother, mother, and child."

"Oh, my!"

Onashola hung her head. She gathered the shawl around her shoulders.

"Is it all right if she stays at the house with me?"

"Of course. Both of you are welcome as long as you want to stay. I told you. I don't use that house. It is yours."

"I can work tomorrow."

"Tomorrow is Sunday, so the library is closed. Why don't you come over for dinner tomorrow night?"

The house was a half-mile from the library, on the same street, on the dirt road north that went all the way to Canada. Betty Pettigrew lived in a large white house with four white columns her husband built from a drawing of a Georgian house he saw when he was a soldier on Sherman's march through Georgia. Brave Eagle's smaller ranch home was built to be a servant's quarters. Betty lived alone in the mansion, with six bedrooms. She employed two servants: a German cook, Johanna, who doubled as a housemaid, and her husband, Gregor, who cared for the four horses and served as a sort of handyman/carpenter. Gregor had served with Mrs. Pettigrew's husband in the Civil War. The couple resided in the town and worked at the mansion on weekdays.

Brave Eagle escorted Onashola into the smaller house, a cozy place, with an open hearth. He built a fire.

"How do you know this woman?" Onashola asked. She sat in one of the two rocking chairs that faced the fireplace, as Brave Eagle fanned the flames.

"From the library."

Brave Eagle had lent Onashola books on occasion. That stopped after she married. Her husband did not approve of her reading, since he could not read and did not trust the English words. She looked at a big, thick book on the floor and picked it up.

"Moby Dick."

"The story of a man chasing a whale. I have yet to start. I thought this would be good, although it is quite long and will take a month to read."

' "I never read a book this big."

Onashola stared into the burning logs.

"I fell. I looked at my son and blood soaked the papoose and his head hung. But the soldiers ran at us, and I ran. My arm ached. The bullet went right through my arm, in one side and out the other. If I did not run fast, they would have killed me. The women with small children, they killed them all. Two, three, and four year olds running with their mothers and shot in the back. What kind of man shoots women and children? What kind of man?"

"Our fathers were white men."

Onashola continued, "They screamed out, "remember Custer! Remember Custer. I remember Wounded Knee, that' is what I remember. I will never be the same. "

They shared a connection to Custer. Brave Eagle was the brave who killed the golden haired general at Little Big Horn, and Onashola, whose mother was one of the captives at Winoshau, a village Custer's army stormed through. There, Custer earned the moniker, "Indian fighter," although of the 103 Indians killed, only 11 were men, the rest women and children. Onashola's mother, Leaping Deer, was spared because of her beauty. After being brought to the fort, the soldiers argued over who could have her. Mrs. Custer ordered Leaping Deer expelled from the fort when she became pregnant and refused to name the father of what would be Onashola. But Leaping Deer knew his identity, and the man died at Little Big Horn. So, Onashola's father died at Little Big Horn, while her mother perished at Wounded Knee. And Brave Eagle fought at Little Big Horn, and lost his wife at Wounded Knee. It was entirely possible that brave Eagle unknowingly killed Onashola's father, for Custer was not his only victim.

Brave Eagle rocked in his chair. Despair revisits. He told Shaded Feather of the death of her sons at Little Big Horn and she went from unhappy to the walking dead, and now poor Onashola. Was it his fate to care for wounded women? She was always a bright, optimistic girl; full of energy and now her spirit was crushed. He struggled himself to find reason in his life, why he had so few moments of joy.

Brave Eagle was by nature a man who looked at the good in things, who counted the things he had rather than what he had not. That was what he appreciated in the young Onashola, always positive, always humble about her considerable physical talents and strengths.

He first was aware of her in the tribe when she was a mere four years of age – the happy girl who could hang from a tree branch and swing her legs for an unusually long time. As she grew, whenever he had the occasion he found ways to teach her tricks with knives, ropes and archery. Her mother looked kindly at Brave Eagle's interest in her daughter. He was a kind and honest man whom everybody knew had an unfortunate mate.

By the time she was seventeen, she had developed into an absolutely stunning beauty and despite her half-breed heritage, the braves clamored for her attention. There was a significant moment where Brave Eagle's conception of his young protégé changed significantly. He stalked an antelope near a creek that day and Onashola emerged from the creek naked. Their eyes locked and Brave Eagle stood still. Onashola backed into the creek and sunk to her knees so he could not see her body and she motioned with her head for him to move on. What he had seen was enough for him to never think of her as a child again, to dream of her.

He tried to beat back desirous thoughts. After all, she was thirty years younger and should find a mate appropriate for her age. What he saw was a lushness of life, as if the prefect woman had been constructed and that she was as far as he was concerned. He did not want to ponder about the vision of the maid emerging from the creek, but many nights that was all he could see.

Neither spoke of that moment for a long time. They went on as before, at least tried to, but Brave Eagle became intensely jealous of all the suitors Onashola inspired. When a particular young brave appeared to be gaining her attention, Brave Eagle discreetly warned Onashola's mother and hoped the mother would end the tryst.

Onashola sometimes sensed Brave Eagle's presence and after one afternoon spent kissing a young boy passionately, she came away ashamed and more worried that Brave Eagle might find out than her own mother. They had some kind of connection that went beyond the locking of eyes by the creek.

CHAPTER 2

❧

As the ground thawed, ever so slowly, from the frozen Dakota earth Onashola's spirits returned. Spring flowers sprung overnight through the hard soil and brought a lift to the depression of winter. Betty Pettigrew gave her a wardrobe, and Onashola traded her buckskin dress for the current South Dakota fashion of white collared blouses, full-length skirts and petticoats. Similarly, Brave Eagle inherited a closet full of the late Mr. Pettigrew's clothes. They gradually assimilated into Rapid City.

Brave Eagle's job at the library was to simply return the books to their shelves. In the morning, he sorted the books, taking the non-fiction and dividing them into the 9 first digits of the Dewey system, and fiction books he divided into four stacks A through F, G through L, M through R, and S through Z. After shelving, he read the newspaper and a book. He read books about Custer and marveled at the inaccuracy of the accounts and how they turned a fool into a martyr. He considered writing the authors and telling them all the correct details, but that would only call more attention to the blonde fool, so he stifled the urge.

Charles Dickens' books made him want to visit London. Once he decided to read every work of fiction in the library, beginning with the As, but some of the books were not worth reading, so he discarded that system in favor of getting recommendations from Mrs. Pettigrew and a few of the regular patrons of the library.

Brave Eagle and Onashola were not the only Native Americans who lived in the white world of Rapid City. About one hundred scattered about the town, in various occupations, trying to mind their own business. Brave Eagle developed a friendship with a Comanche named

Tilted Sun and sometimes they huddled outside of the general store, sitting in rocking chairs and watching the wagons go by.

Rapid City sprang up after the gold rush, but the population had declined to a little over a thousand as many of the miners had given up on finding any more gold. The city was arranged in six blocks, with the library on the northwestern edge.

"Here we are, living like white men," Tilted Sun said one time.

"It's better than life on the reservation," Brave Eagle commented.

Tilted Sun nodded.

"My father would be angry with me. He hated them." Tilted Sun added.

"My father was white, but I think he was more comfortable with our people," Brave Eagle said. 'There are some good, some bad, the same as it is with us. At least, here, life is more comfortable."

They could not enter many of the establishments in the city. The saloons were off limits. The general store, the library, one hotel (not the other), and the six-bed hospital welcomed them. They were not welcome at the local brothel.

Onashola assisted in the stables. Her chores took a couple of hours each day, when she typically returned to the house to read the "women's" books Brave Eagle brought from the library. Her favorite authors included the Bronte sisters, Jane Austen and Louisa May Alcott.

Brave Eagle's feelings for Onashola changed as her brightness returned. He was reluctant to take her into town, where some young man might flirt with her and try to take her away.

His feelings increased day by day. When he returned from a day at the library, she greeted him with excitement, to tell him of the latest adventures in books. She prepared a meal, and they talked for hours about the twists and turns of their own lives.

Onashola slept on the bed only six feet from Brave Eagle, in a white linen nightgown Betty Pettigrew provided, while he slept in a red nightshirt.

One night of a full moon, Brave Eagle noticed Onashola's blanket had shifted and in the light he saw her bare bottom. He fought urges of desire.

He considered ravaging her and worrying about the consequences later, but he wanted her to stay with him.

He made up his mind. He would get into her bed and hold her. If she pushed him away, he would say he worried she was cold. He expected rejection. But, he took the two paces and slid into her bed. Her back was to him and he carefully slid into the bed and her body heat increased his breathing. He was aware of her behind against his thighs. After ten minutes of holding his breath and not moving, he lifted his nightshirt so his right leg touched her rear. The excitement of contact with her skin caused him to breathe deeply, and involuntarily he became aroused. He tried to think about other things, like fishing or running through the fields, anything to dampen his growing need, when she moved. Almost imperceptibly and with her back still to him, she opened her legs, and Brave Eagle moved his right leg between her legs.

She reached her hand under his nightshirt, held him in her hand and with one smooth stroke, inserted him.

He gripped her firm thighs. Onashola moaned and talked as her passion rose. "That is the way," she cried. Brave Eagle had not been with a talking woman in bed and it excited him all the more. He was accustomed to passivity, to "This is my duty," and not one of uncontrollable desire.

She kissed him and grasped his hand. "All is good now. I am yours and you are mine."

"From this moment on."

She rested in the nook of his shoulder. From the depths of tragedy, a time in which both he and Onashola lost everything, he gained something - a life partner.

This began a period of brightness in which Brave Eagle awoke every morning and said a prayer of thanks. A quickness returned to his step and he considered he was in better condition than most men twenty years his junior.

Onashola had always loved and revered Brave Eagle. She never thought of him as an endearing family friend or as a mentor. She considered him the ideal man and when she found a mate, she wanted someone to fit his image. Never did she dream that she would marry Brave Eagle.

Onashola's mother, Walking Flower, suffered much abuse when Custer's wife Libbie expelled her from the fort, four months into the pregnancy. She was spat upon and had rocks hurled at her by other women, with venomous insults shouted at her. If not for the stature of her father, a medicine man, she would have been expelled from the tribe completely.

The child also experienced insults from other children about her father and whoring mother. But as time wore on, her beauty and superior abilities overcame this prejudice and taints were replaced by jealousy.

The father she never knew was Lieutenant Michael Ford. Leaping Deer told her daughter of her father and his death at Little Big Horn. Michael was born and raised in Chicago. Too young from the Civil War, he enlisted in the cavalry at 18 in 1867. His intelligence and leadership qualities resulted in an officer's commission and he was promoted to first lieutenant shortly before Little Big Horn.

Michael's passion was the game of chess and he traveled with a board in his satchel, teaching any man with the mildest interest in learning the game. However, the ability to think one move ahead did not apply to Custer. Michael thought of battles in chess terms, and as the armies of the Sioux closed in upon him, all he could think was "Checkmate."

He instructed Leaping Deer in chess, too and perhaps his approach to courtship was more polite and less forward than the other soldiers, who thought nothing of groping her. She narrowly averted rape several times in the fort and the officer's wives heard that all the men's attentions were centered upon one beautiful Indian maiden.

The one day of intimacy Leaping Deer shared with Michael Ford happened on a day when most of the soldiers were away on patrol and he was given an off duty day. The officer's barracks were empty and they found a bed. They never had another opportunity, and the best they could do after that was a touch of hands while passing near each other, a smile and acknowledgement. Michael told Leaping Deer that he would marry her as soon as his term ended in South Dakota and that they must remain discreet to avoid suspicion. It was Libbie Custer who detected the pregnancy and had her kicked out of the fort. The officer's wives had clamored for her expulsion for months, as even their husbands took an interest in that "one squaw."

After the Battle of Little Big Horn, the remnants of the soldier's possessions were displayed to the tribe and there, in the midst of a pile of rubble, Leaping Deer picked out the Queen from a chess set. That queen stayed with her until her death at Wounded Knee. What Leaping Deer could tell Onashola about her father that he was a kind and intelligent man, a man who read and wrote poetry and was very unlike the rough soldiers at the fort. If there was any lesson she learned it was that all whites were not savages. But many of them were. The white men all seemed consumed with lust, which seemed natural since only a few of the officer's wives lived there and the noncommissioned men were not allowed to house their wives at the fort. Most of the men were unmarried and a great many of them, virgins who panted like dogs at the mere sight of a woman.

Michael Ford's father was a Union Colonel, killed at Gettysburg. His mother a teacher. He was the oldest of three sons and Onashola had no idea that she had six cousins living in Illinois.

Sometimes growing up, she spent more time with Brave Eagle than with the children of her own age and more than one squaw mentioned to Shaded Feather that they wondered if Brave Eagle ha an unnatural in-clination towards Onashola, trying to stir gossip. Shaded Feather knew the accusation was preposterous and defended her husband by observing that for one thing, he could understand what being a half-breed meant and he also had a mentoring way about him. He had married her even though she had two sons and did his best to replace their late father. Many braves would have balked at the prospect of marrying a widow with children, but Brave Eagle took it on.

It was well recognized that Onashola was the most coveted of all the young women and would overcome her stigma in finding a mate. With all the attention, for a while, she relished it and appeared to lead several boys on at the same time, all thinking she was in love with them. She grew angry with Brave Eagle when he accused her of toying with boys like a cat with a mouse and the feud lasted for a year. She knew Brave Eagle disapproved of several of her suitors and intentionally paraded them in front of him, seeing if she could get a reaction.

Betty was the first to detect that Onashola was pregnant, knowing the signs. At her insistence, Brave Eagle and Onashola married before the justice of the piece, to make their union official in the white world. Brave Eagle adopted the name, "Thomas Heard," and Onashola became Onashola Heard. Her belly grew and the very site filled Brave Eagle with awe. Shaded Feather had a couple ill-fated pregnancies that ended before he ever knew they began. This time, Onashola progressed naturally and Brave Eagle often put his hand upon her stomach to detect the growing fetus. It did not seem possible, for he had long before discarded the possibility that he would father a child. One night, he muttered to Onashola as they lay in bed,

"From tragedy comes new life."

"Yes. I think that many times," Onashola agreed.

"We can not take this blessing for granted."

"This child wants to live."

"I am honored to father this child, girl or boy. Here I was, retiring to a life as a library assistant. A warrior who counted coups many times, shelving books. Now I have a purpose."

Growing inside of Onashola was Maka. Maka, a Lakota name that meant, "Earth Goddess," was an especially long infant. The hospital nurse measured her as thirty inches at birth. It surprised both of her parents, although Brave Eagle's father was six feet four inches tall.

She was born in January of 1892. Benjamin Harrison of Indiana was President of the States, about to be defeated for re-election by a former president, Grover Cleveland. Harrison had spoiled Cleveland's bid for re-election in 1888 and Cleveland wanted the White House back. Brave Eagle and Onashola voted for the first time, for Harrison.

Maka changed the daily routines. Betty Pettigrew released Onashola of her duties at the house so she could attend to the baby, who woke several times. It was eight months before she slept through the night.

"What part Lakota and what part white is Maka if we are half of each?" Onashola asked. "If you multiply a half times a half you get one fourth, so are they one fourth Lakota now?"

Whatever her mix, Maka was a beautiful infant with tanned skin and her mother's silky black hair. Her parents planned that she would learn all their skills: archery, knife throwing, wrestling, and running. She also would inherit their love of reading, and attend college. Betty Pettigrew had a piano and she would be trained. They discussed moving to a warmer climate like Arizona, but home was Rapid City. Brave Eagle realized he had to maintain his health if he wanted to experience his daughter's growth.

Onashola treasured her infant almost too much, having lost her first one, she was protective. Brave Eagle called her "Momma Bear," the way she looked out for her cub.

Maka slept in a small crib by their bedside and often Brave Eagle gazed upon the sleeping infant and wondered aloud, "Onashola. Can you believe it?"

He was, a man in his fifties, with his own small baby for the first time. Some men in his tribe showed open disappointment if they had a daughter and not a son. It did not matter to Brave Eagle. Not long before, he had nothing but a three-legged dog, Bone, who guarded the crib zealously. He was not the oldest man to father a child, He was not even sure of his age; he was born the same year as Crazy Horse, when-ever that was.

Men still came to South Dakota in search of gold, gave up and became saloonkeepers, hotel desk clerks, and accountants. Gold, after all, brought Custer to the Black hills, to claim it for the United States and take more land away from the Indians. Brave Eagle steered clear of the saloons, where trouble often brewed.

He wanted to live to be 100 years old. Not many did, but old White Cloud on the reservation, was rumored to bed two women at a time into his eighties. They said White Cloud died with a big smile on his face and his women cried profuse tears at his passing.

Brave Eagle ran to and from the library, carrying books. When he did not work, he found ways for physical activity, stacking hay in the barn, unstacking, and stacking. He hung on a post in the barn and extended his thighs straight out, holding the position for an hour.

He practiced throwing his knife at targets and hunted with bow and arrow, bringing in enough meat to feed his family without having to pay a butcher. Sometimes Onashola went with him on the hunt, carrying Maka on her back. They intended for Maka to become a woman who could defend herself. With idiot cowboys coming into town, it was best a woman knew self-defense. Although Brave Eagle had his foot in both the white and red worlds, he felt red at heart, a red man, learning to survive. He longed for an Indian Dickens, or a Twain to describe the travails of the life they led.

As Maka started walking, Brave Eagle detected a swell in Onashola's stomach and rested his hand there one night. She nodded.

"Another."

Another was about to join the family! Wishiwu would be born close to Maka's second birthday, in March, when the snow melted. Betty Pettigrew often served as a baby sitter for Maka, and was excited about another arrival. She had the world of books as a substitute for children. Her husband, Mike Pettigrew, was an astute businessman. He owned a newspaper and a shipping business on the Chicago River. When rumors of gold in South Dakota rang out, he set out on his own with mining equipment. One year later, he came back a rich man and moved his wife, Betty, to Rapid City. After getting what he could, he dynamited his mine and tried to leave no trace. He built the two houses, a barn a half dozen horses. They built the library for Betty to pursue her passion. Mike Pettigrew was not even forty years old when he died.

Of course, the locals suspected Indians, whenever there was much unrest. But the murder went unsolved. Betty was alone, and she employed the two servants to help out at the house and with the horses. She became very fond of Brave Eagle, the book lover, and was somewhat taken aback when he returned with the young woman, Onashola. She expected a romantic relationship would develop between Brave Eagle and Onashola once she got to know Onashola and realized she was so much like Brave Eagle. Betty once saw Onashola stalk a rabbit, capture, kill and skin it. She was happy to have them right next door, though.

After her husband's death, Betty Pettigrew took the train to San Francisco and deposited eighty thousand dollars in a bank, keeping forty in Rapid City. She suspected the map of his mine in the Black Hills was the cause of Mike's death. She kept the map in the box in San Francisco, with no intention of unveiling it. If he had drawn gold from the hills, it was not his, anyway, since the land rightfully belonged to the Sioux. All she knew was he had made money in Chicago with his shipping and newspapers, she still owned them and an accountant deposited profits into a growing account. After Maka's birth, an attorney drew up her will. If Brave Eagle and Onashola survived her, they would get half of her assets, and their child or children the other half. She had no other family.

Wishiwu was born in March of 1894. It was a hard delivery for Onashola and poor Bone howled at the front door as his mistress screamed in pain. But Onashola made it through the delivery.

The doctor pulled Brave Eagle aside shortly after the birth,

"She can't have another," he whispered.

"I never imagined having another child. I am not at all greedy for more!"

He realized by the time his daughters were of childbearing age, he would be ancient, so he increased his efforts to stay healthy. He did not want his grandchildren to come up to a wrinkled old man covered in blankets, one who did not even know who he was.

Wishiwu could have passed for Maka's twin. Maka asserted herself in the daughter hierarchy, as the lead dog in this family, and Wishiwu learned from her. By the time Maka was six years old, she could string a bow and shoot an arrow into a mark on a tree fifty yards away. She could hurl a knife from twenty yards and hit the target. She was such a swift runner; it took Brave Eagle twenty yards to get enough traction to over-take her. Wishiwu was the clown, while Maka was more serious. Betty Pettigrew taught them to read, and at six, Maka could name the capitals of every state and count to one thousand. As far as their culture and heritage, the girls learned of the red man's way from their parents, but they grew up in the white world. When his daughters interacted with other children in Rapid City, Brave Eagle and Onashola noticed their daughters demon-strated maturity far beyond their years. Onashola commented that Maka was born a twenty year old, assisting her little sister in getting dressed in the morning, taking her to the outhouse in the yard

Their lives changed dramatically. The other survivors of Wounded Knee returned to reservation life, while Brave Eagle and Onashola inte-grated into Rapid City. They did not turn their backs on who they were, but neither had any family left and few surviving friends. Only once had Onashola seen someone from the reservation, a woman whose husband found employment at the hotel. Although their house was small, it was a mansion compared to living in a teepee.

The library continued to bring in books that satisfied Brave Eagle and Onashola's hunger for reading. They devoured the Sherlock Holmes books written by Arthur Conan Doyle, and the Thomas Hardy novels of an England they longed to visit. Brave Eagle enjoyed Sherlock Holmes so much; he discussed leaving the library for the excitement of joining the sheriff's department. Onashola would not hear of it. The sheriff mostly dealt with drunks, and there had been a bank robbery with a shootout. Every weekend, the ranch hands came into the town and caused trouble. The library was the safest place to be on those days.

Onashola gloried in the miracle of her two children and every Sunday attended Catholic Mass to give thanks. She never forgot her Little One, though, the little boy whose spirit never had a chance to soar. The Catholics did not believe in reincarnation, but the Indians did, and so did Onashola. A spirit might return as an animal, or as another person. She looked for signs of Little One in her daughters. She still kept the papoose, packed away in a box, but still in her heart. At night, she got down on her knees in prayer. Brave Eagle did not get down on his knees. He believed in Jesus because he saw Jesus himself, on his Vision Quest, when he set off to the Black Butte for a week long fast. He only told the reservation Priest of his visit from Jesus, and the priest said it was delirium. But he did see him, at the moment an Eagle flew over his head, he sat on a hilltop and looked down upon the land and Jesus reached out and held his hand. This happened before Wounded Knee, even before he met Shaded Feather. He took it to mean everything in his life would be right. But he lost everything first.

He also believed in his Indian religion, too and believed a fusion as the best way to live. Looking over the sequence of events, the desire for the return of Jesus led to the Ghost Dance, to Wounded Knee, and for Brave Eagle, Onashola, Maka and Wishiwu. If not for the Ghost Dance, he would not have found happiness, for his joy sprang from tragedy.

The Priest told Brave Eagle not to tell anyone else of seeing Jesus, lest they think he was crazy, so he never did. Not even to Onashola. Why had he been singled out? Brave Eagle did not crave at all for attention, unlike his friend Crazy Horse. If Jesus rose from the dead, Brave Eagle could go from nothing to something. Yet his daughters made him wonder if they had supernatural powers. They were way beyond the physical talent of his own boyhood and he was considered, along with Crazy Horse, far above the other braves in skills. Maybe his daughters were Chosen Ones.

One day in July, three drunken cowboys confronted Onashola outside of the general store. Brave Eagle had gone to the blacksmith to reshod a horse.

"Look at the pretty squaw! I found me a squaw, boys!" One of the cowboys, a freckled man with a scar across his cheek stood in Onashola's path as she carried a bag of flour. The other cowboys moved in behind her.

"I must get by," Onashola protested.

"What's that in the bag, squaw?" The freckled cowboy smiled at her with his rotted teeth, besotted with alcohol.

"Flour. Please let me by. My husband is waiting."

"Let me see," one of the cowboys grabbed the flour and threw it to the ground, its white contents spilling out.

"OH, what we done did! "

Onashola stooped down to scoop the flour into the bag.

"Let me help you," the cowboy grabbed a handful of flour from the ground.

"You could be a little whiter," and he reached down and smeared it over Onashola's face.

"Stop! " she shoved him so he fell backward to the ground.

"Well, I'll. You don't do that to me. Boys hold the Indian."

The two thugs grabbed her and held her as she struggled and the freckled cowboy slapped her across the face. He slapped once and pre-pared to backhand her, when a whip cracked and the man shrieked.

Brave Eagle stood alone in the street, holding a horsewhip. The men let Onashola go and one of them reached for a pistol in his holster, when the whip slapped his wrist and the gun fell. The other man moved away and raised his arms like he wanted no part of the fight. Onashola picked the remains of the flour bag from the ground and ran from the men and behind Brave Eagle.

"Bastard Indians," the freckled man shouted. "I'll show you,"

"Don't do it!' Brave Eagle warned.

But the stupid freckled man did. He reached for his gun and Brave Eagle's whip flashed, this time across the man's face, and he rushed at the howling man, pulling his Bowie knife from its sheath. He sat on top of the man, knife to his throat. Onashola retrieved the pistol from the ground, cocked and aimed at the other cowboys, who stepped away.

"I took the scalp of men much better than you," Brave Eagle warned.

"Take mine, too you stupid half-breed!" the man spit on Brave Eagle, despite the knife to his throat. Brave Eagle reached back and sliced the man's Achilles tendons. First the left, then the right.

"Now, walk." Brave Eagle got up from the man, who stood and attempted a step, but crumpled back to the ground. The other cowboys helped the limp man away.

"We will be back!' he yelled.

A crowd gathered, and huddled around Brave Eagle and Onashola in the street. Sheriff Thompson, a rough character who squinted because he refused to wear glasses, arrived.

"What was that all about?"

"Those men hit Onashola. So I stopped them. They had guns, but they don't any more."

"I'll take the guns," the Sheriff said, reaching out. "Who were they?"

"New ranch hands for McEver," one of the bystanders commented.

Leo McEver was the wealthiest man in South Dakota. He owned mines in the Black Hills, 20,000 acres outside of Rapid City, all the saloons, a thirty-room hotel and a large ranch with livestock. He spent much of his time in San Francisco, preferring to wait out the frigid winters, when he returned to his Dakota ranch in April.

Sheriff Thompson shrugged. McEver funded the judge's pocketbooks. He hired ranch workers who were out of step with the law, and it was a good thing he housed them on his ranch, away from town. But weekends they came into town, got drunk, were serviced by the four prostitutes at the brothel, and sometimes spent a night or two in jail.

Brave Eagle and Onashola returned to their home. The commotion in town upset Onashola and as soon as they stepped into their house, she threw up.

Brave Eagle started a fire and they sat at the fireplace.

"They wouldn't bother you if you were ugly. Black Elk claimed an ugly woman brings fewer problems than a beautiful one."

"Would you rather I be ugly?"

He reached for her hand.

"What are you going to do when I am old and feeble, walking with a cane?"

"To me, you will always be my man. When you are old, I will be older, too."

"Ha. Not nearly as old as me! And some young bucks will try to take you away from me."

"Oh stop. I glory in my fortune every day. And always will."

Their fortunes were about to change. The skirmish with McEver's men was only a hint of what was yet to come.

CHAPTER 3

Crazy Horse

CHARLES HEARD, BARTERED with Indians, trading guns, whiskey, horses, and various relics for Buffalo skins, buckskins, anything of value he could salvage. Heard was a native of Minnesota, the descendent of a member of the Lewis and Clark expedition. He grew up near the Mississippi, and gravitated towards that river and hired on as a boatman on a riverboat. Over time, he met many Indians and found a comfort with their customs and acquired the art of trading goods along the riverbanks. After accumulating a big haul of goods to trade, several Sioux escorted him into their midst where he was welcomed and befriended. He traded a dozen horses to White Cloud for his daughter, Hopping Mouse, the most beautiful girl in the tribe. This created a great deal of friction amongst tribe members, so White Cloud distributed six of the horses to other tribesman.

Heard lived on and off with Hopping Mouse, and the child, Brave Eagle. He mingled with the tribes effortlessly because he had learned to speak their language and was a constant source of supplies. Brave Eagle's father taught him how to survive the taunts of other children because he was a half-breed. His father told him he had a destiny far greater than any of the other children. When Brave Eagle was eleven, his father did not return from one of his trading jaunts. His body was found after the spring thaw, a skeleton full of Crow arrows.

Brave Eagle kept to himself. The tribe followed the buffalo and moved camps and there was no reservation. One boy, a bully named Shooting Arrow, a massive boy in height and girth, a head taller than the other boys and fond of hurling insults and intimidating children into surrendering their possessions, whether they be knives, moccasins, or precious stones. Brave Eagle avoided him, and maintained his composure when Shooting Arrow called him a lowly half-breed. But Shooting Arrow could not fluster Brave Eagle and sought other targets. One day, Shooting Arrow went too far and stalked Brave Eagle with two other boys. They walked behind him, and Shooting Arrow said Brave Eagle was the son of a white man's whore.

Though only twelve years old and about one hundred pounds, Brave Eagle punched Shooting Arrow with such force, his fist hitting the jaw, Shooting Arrow lifted off the ground and fell unconscious. Word spread about Brave Eagle's strength, and since Shooting Arrow was very unpopular, he became a silent boy hero.

However, everyone knew the prize child in the tribe was Crazy Horse, the most agile, swiftest, and strongest, and undoubtedly a future leader of the tribe. Crazy Horse was a couple inches taller than Brave Eagle and slender. He was quite unique with his curly hair, so that he was called, "Curly." He had a tremendous ego and when the other children talked about the courageous Brave Eagle, he figured it was a time to show everyone he indeed was the most gifted. He organized a bout of "Knock them off their horses," a tournament in which the boys rode horses and tried to knock the others off their mounts. The last boy still on the horse would be the victor.

The tournament took place one sweltering July day, and most of the tribe formed a big circle to spectate. Fifteen youths joined in the fray. Brave Eagle knew without any doubt, no one could knock him off his mount. He fixed his eyes upon the exact point he would jut out his arm and hit his opponent with such force they flew backwards to the ground. The key was to gather momentum. Brave Eagle pushed five of the horse boys to the ground. Then, the last brave left was Crazy Horse. They charged at each other, but Crazy Horse observed Brave Eagle's method and at the last second, dodged and evaded the thrust. Brave Eagle realized he had a smarter adversary this time around. The second pass, Brave Eagle missed again and Crazy Horse slapped him in the face as he passed, leaving a stinging red welt.

Brave Eagle had enough and decided to end the joust, but Crazy Horse was as convinced it was time to count coup. Brave Eagle kicked his horse in the ribs to gain speed and charged. They met with such force and fury that both were sent flying off their horses. The match was declared a tie and both presented tomahawks.

Crazy Horse spoke to Brave Eagle afterwards.

"I thought no one could get me off my horse."

"I too," Brave Eagle replied.

Crazy Horse believed he was invincible, bullets could never wound him, and spirits protected him from harm. Brave Eagle also would go into battles with the same belief. They fought several battles together and with others dying around them, neither one would ever be touched.

In the last rush against the 7th cavalry, only the long yellow hair and two other men stood amongst the dead and dying. Custer saw Brave Eagle and Crazy Horse coming and he was out of bullets and he gasped. Brave Eagle later wished they let Custer walk back alone. That way he would not turn into the martyr that would signal the end of the Sioux way of life.

Crazy Horse led that charge, as he always did, leading his men some 30 yards to the front on horseback, a war club in one hand and a rifle in the other. Brave Eagle rode in the next wave, knowing it best to allow Crazy Horse to take the front. Crazy Horse was a terrifying figure, periodically blowing a terrifying shrieking sound from his horn. Brave Eagle thought that he too would be afraid of such a warrior advancing upon him. That day, Brave Eagle followed as Crazy Horse swooped down with his club, smashing skulls left and right. He killed thirty-one of the soldiers. Brave Eagle did not keep track of how many soldiers he put down. Little Big Horn was Brave Eagle's last battle, and Custer the last man he killed. There were many battles before with the soldiers and Crows. Fighting was part of existence. Fighting and women.

Before Onashola, Brave Eagle never experienced the quickening of the pulse, the beating of the heart, all the signs of a man in love. His first effort at courtship was with a girl he later called She Devil. Her actual name was Flowing Creek, and several others courted her. She told Brave Eagle she loved him, but she also loved Tall Brook.

Brave Eagle learned she lost her virginity to Tall Brook. She could not make up her mind and even suggested she would welcome sleeping with both of them. Brave Eagle thought she was crazy and walked away, as did Tall Brook. She later moved on and married a Shoshone.

The Sioux did not practice marriage in the white man's meaning of the word. One shared a tipi and if the relationship soured, all it took was to place all the clothes and possessions outside and the offended party found another tipi.

Brave Eagle had a string of courtships after Sticking Tree, but none developed, and when Shaded Feather widowed, her two boys needed a patriarch and he filled the role. Shaded Feather had a series of miscarriages, so Brave Eagle's chances to father a child were over. Other women tempted him while living with Shaded Feather, but he resignedly admitted this was his lot in life. What he did not anticipate was the depth of her unhappiness. When he began his courtship, she was warm and friendly and appeared happy, until the day he moved in. Her morose attitude grew, and, after the two boys were killed at Little Big Horn, she became almost comatose with depression, a depression that would last the dozen years until her death at Wounded Knee.

Crazy Horse was not much luckier with his romantic forays. An irate husband shot him for taking his wife away, and almost killed him. If not for one incident, Crazy Horse would have been Chief. His fearlessness in battle led to his being named Shirt Wearer, or war chief. He saw visions of the Spirit World and a white owl in that world. Prior to any battle, he entered a trance-like state in which he was in that world with the white owl at his side. In that state, he entered battles knowing he would not be hurt. He painted a yellow lightning bolt on his face, and dusted with white powder.

Brave Eagle had a similar sensation and was in every fight with Crazy Horse. He visualized passing through the enemy, untouched. Crazy Horse sought out engagement within the battle and killed more adversaries than anyone else. Crazy Horse's main purpose was in killing, while Brave Eagle's was in surviving. Before the attack, Brave Eagle always said a Bible verse to himself, "Yay, though I walk through the valley of death, I will fear no evil." One particular moment in a fight haunted him, in the Battle of the Rosebud, only one week before Little Big Horn; he came upon a young soldier who lost his horse and was wounded in the leg. The young man held up his hands and said, "Please, please, I have children." Brave Eagle kicked his horse on, hearing the shots behind him of a brave killing the man. He had been warned never to feel empathy for your enemy. But the night after the battle, Brave Eagle thought of the man's children and was very sad.

Crazy Horse was charismatic and the braves idolized him. So, too, did the women. He was startlingly handsome and had penetrating black eyes. Black Buffalo Woman, the wife of No Water, openly flirted with Crazy Horse, and he invited her to go on a buffalo hunt at a time her husband left the village for a hunt. When No Water returned and learned his wife had left, he tracked them down.

He found Crazy Horse and Black Buffalo Woman together in a tipi, and pulled out his pistol. Crazy Horse's friend Touch of the Clouds saw No Water enter the tent and arrived in time to deflect the pistol, but it still shot Crazy Horse in the jaw. No Water demanded compensation from the elders of the tribe.

Although Crazy Horse was the prized warrior, they ruled he could never become Chief and never live with Black Buffalo Woman. No Water gave Crazy Horse three horses.

Instead, Crazy Horse married Black Short, and had one child, They Are Not Afraid of Her, who only lived three years. Crazy Horse grew dissatisfied over time with Black Short and added a second wife, Nellie, as the Sioux had no rule against such an arrangement.

Crazy Horse always counted on Brave Eagle in a fight because he, too, was not afraid. He considered Brave Eagle a friend, though he was still not one of the inner circle. Brave Eagle did not plan battles. He fought them. There was always the issue of his parentage, a half-breed.

After Little Big Horn, the soldiers took revenge by attacking a Miconjou village and killing every man, woman, and child, over one hundred. A harsh winter made surrender inevitable, for starvation faced the tribe, and Crazy Horse surrendered to Fort Robinson. Brave Eagle went with Crazy Horse, because he spoke English so well, He saw a soldier reading a book, The Scarlet Letter, and Brave Eagle asked if he could trade for some books. The man returned with a box of books and told Brave Eagle to take his pick.

A few months later, members of the tribe told the soldiers Crazy Horse planned to go back on the warpath, and he was arrested. As they tried to arrest him inside the fort, he wrestled with the soldier and another Indian, Little Big Man, and was bayoneted to death in the struggle. He prepared for a battle by entering his spirit world, but that didn't help him in this case.

In losing Crazy Horse, the Sioux lost their inspirational figure, the one with the fighting spirit. But Brave Eagle was weary of fighting, and listening to his wife wail over the death of her sons. He retreated into the world of his books. At least in this fictional world, one found peace and harmony. At times he thought about leaving the tribe, leaving his wife. He might cut his hair and wear white man's clothes and fit right in, well, almost. His dark toned skin revealed he was not completely white. All this fuss the country made about freeing the black slaves, yet the color of the skin still mattered. Over the years, Brave Eagle ignored many insults. They did not know he could kill them with his bare hands.

Brave Eagle found regular employment as a translator over treaty discussions. He was surprised at the audacity of the Homestead Act gave Americans the right to own 160 acres of land if they lived on the land for five years. Why were they surprised when the Indians fought back?

Brave Eagle first met Onashola when she was six years old, kicking a ball around by herself and kicked the ball over to Brave Eagle, who sat in front of his tipi in his customary position, immersed in a book.

She was dressed in a buckskin skirt and moccasins. Some of the children wore the clothes of the white settlers who donated their old clothes to them, but on this particular day Onashola was clad in Indian dress. Brave Eagle took one look at her and detected she was of mixed heritage.

"What are you reading?"

"Ivanhoe by Walter Scott."

"I can read."

"Oh?"

"I go to the school," she pointed to the nearby fort, as at that time a good number of the tribe lived within a half mile of the fort. To some Indians, they called themselves Hang Around the Fort Indians. But they found it much easier than their typical nomadic life of chasing the buffalo around the west.

"Good. You will learn fast."

"What's the book about?"

"Oh, men in Scotland many years ago."

"Where's Scotland?"

"Across the ocean, by England."

"I've never seen the ocean."

"I haven't either. But I want to someday."

"Me, too. I don't want to stay here."

Brave Eagle knew what she went through, being a shunned half-breed himself. That simple conversation led to many, and Brave Eagle became her teacher of many skills.

When she grew to be a beautiful teenaged girl, the boys started hanging around and that bothered Brave Eagle. When she told him about one boyfriend, he felt jealous.

"Be careful, Onashola. Don't let him take advantage of you. Many men will desire you, so you have time to choose."

"I love this one. He wants to marry me."

"Marry you? You are only fifteen. That would be the end of your life."

"You are married, Brave Eagle. "

"Yes, and it is the end of my life."

He was surprised he said that. Onashola looked surprised. "What do you mean?"

"Can you keep a secret?"

"Yes." She sat down next to him and he put his hand on her shoulder.

"I fought many battles. The joy I get from going into these books is because I find a world that still matters. I am married to a woman who wants to die. I probably will die before she does. I am surprised she doesn't jump off a mountain or go swimming in the rapids, she wants to die so much."

"Shaded Feather wants to die. But why? She is married to a good man."

"Even before her sons were killed, she had a black cloud in her head. But on that day, when the Lakota were victorious, signaled the end of her life and she awaits death."

"I am sorry for you, Brave Eagle. Why don't you set her out?"

Brave Eagle shrugged. "I ask myself that question, many times. I would so like to hop on one of the trains and go to Chicago, or New York, one of those big cities, and change my life. "

"I would miss you, Brave Eagle. You taught me many things."

"And you are one of the reasons I stay, Onashola."

Much like her mother, Onashola's beauty grew to a degree that men from both her tribe and the fort would stop what they were doing and admire her. Many of the men in the fort whistled and yelled at her when she walked from her lessons.

One day, some of the rougher soldiers tried to corner her before she left the fort. A husky, bearded man who stunk of tobacco stood in front of her and put his hands on her shoulder.

"Hey, squaw, where do you think you are going?"

She held a knife to his groin. "Wherever I want to."

He saw the knife. "Easy now, squaw, I meant no harm" and he stepped away.

Another time, a young man came up to her.

"Excuse me, miss. May I ask your name?"

"Onashola." This one seemed polite, at least, so she stopped to listen, accustomed to the loutish behavior of the soldiers.

"Onashola. A beautiful name. I have seen you coming from the school. I was wondering. I would like to court you, so is it the custom to ask your father's permission?"

"What do you mean by court?"

"Maybe permission to spend a day, picnic by a river. Riding horses for a day. Something like that."

"Not with someone from the fort. I cannot and don't want to. You are a soldier. And that is all I need to know."

"Pardon me, Miss. I thought it permissible."

"You thought wrong."

In her village, braves fought over who could be with Onashola. Two boys had a knife fight over the right to make her their woman and neither of them ever even spoke to her. Brute force never worked with Onashola, because she took care of herself. No one was as good with bow and arrow. No one ran as fast. Not one boy. Brave Eagle taught her how to shoot a six-shooter from a horse by hanging beneath the horse's head, in the way the Lakota fought their battles, using the horse as a shield. She demonstrated her skills in a shooting contest, and at full gallop, hit a target six times. None of the boys hit the target more than once.

One boy won her heart. She was about seventeen when Flat Iron broke relations with his girlfriend to pursue Onashola. All the women in the village swooned over his dashing good looks. He was over six feet, extremely strong and undefeated at wrestling. Onashola was not one of the women who gushed over him and he liked that. He decided she would be the ultimate conquest, since all the other men had failed.

Brave Eagle noticed Onashola was very interested and objected that Flat Iron was illiterate. He was a charismatic leader, however, one who wished for the old ways to return. He wanted to fight the soldiers and that sentiment grew. When Wovoka had his vision in Nevada and it spread to the Oglala tribe, Flat Iron was foremost in the dance.

Brave Eagle disapproved of Flat Iron and it caused a fissure in their relationship. Brave Eagle heard about their upcoming marriage and was very disappointed Onashola did not tell him He saw her one day and called out to her.

"Onashola."

She grimaced. "I'm sorry I did not tell you, but I knew your response."

Brave Eagle shrugged. "You will always be precious to me, Onashola, so I wish you a good life, with many children."

"Thank you, Brave Eagle. You are my spirit guide and that will not change."

"Except in matters of the heart."

She smiled. "Flat Iron makes me happy."

"Good and that is something you deserve."

Brave Eagle was very unhappy when she married. He doubted any man worthy of Onashola. She brought brightness into his life throughout her development, one missing in his own marriage. It made him even unhappier with Shaded Feather, who he tried to coax back into life.

He saw Onashola as he loaded Bone into his carriage to journey to Rapid City while the tribe moved on to Wounded Knee and she made a remark that struck a chord.

"I think in some ways, your retreat into books is like Shaded Feather's retreat into her own head."

That was true. He had given up on living, but loved books. If it was an escape, it was one he craved. He pondered asking Mrs. Pettigrew if he could stay in Rapid City in her guesthouse, and he would give Shaded Feather an ultimatum. That was his plan until Mrs. Pettigrew informed him of the massacre.

Onashola viewed the ghost dance with skepticism, like Brave Eagle, but kept those thoughts to herself because Flat Iron was so convinced the Messiah was about to return and obliterate the white race. Flat Iron didn't consider his own wife was half white, and what would happen to her if they all disappeared?

Onashola was Christian like many in the village, and the new way followed this Messiah as his chosen people. What if Wovoka was right? Onashola doubted it, but the fervor in the tribe grew with each dance. How many times did they dance before it came true?

There was nothing in Wovoka's vision about killing all the whites. They were going to disappear somehow. The word spread throughout all the tribes about a prescribed method to bring this about and it required ghost dancing. The western forts were alerted to what the ghost dances meant and anticipated an uprising, and that led to the massacre at Wounded Knee. The soldiers were there to take all the weapons to prevent the Indians from attacking the fort. Of the many eyewitness versions of why the shooting started, the most cited was Red Cloud's rifle went off when they took it from him, and the tense soldiers opened fire. The tribe returned the fire, but the opening volley killed most of the ones with weapons. Once that happened, and the rest of the tribe ran, the soldiers chased them down and showed no mercy.

Onashola's Little One was only three months old and she worshiped the happy little baby. She could not get over having such a healthy baby, as many of the infants had health problems if they survived birth, and he was a robust infant, born with a full head of black hair. His father, Flat Iron, was convinced he fathered a future Chief.

"With a father of such strength and power, and a mother of such beauty, he will be the next Crazy Horse."

" I love him beyond anything," Onashola told her husband.

Brave Eagle saw the baby only once, when Onashola delivered. He did not care for Flat Iron and the feeling was mutual. As soon as Flat Iron married Onashola, he asserted his position:

"Brave Eagle lives in the pages of those books now. He has a no good wife, so he would rather read about other places. I think he secretly desires you, that is why he hangs around."

"I gain much from Brave Eagle," Onashola protested.

"I don't want you to see him any more."

"But that is not possible. His tipi is only across the field."

"Avoid him. You are mine now. His days are past and he is going to wither."

Onashola never told Brave Eagle her husband forbid for her to see him, she avoided him. One day, Brave Eagle walked over to visit the new husband and wife and was greeted by Flat Iron.

"What are you doing here?"

"I have not seen the new couple since the ceremony. I wanted to visit."

"You came to see Onashola, not me. And she is with her mother. But, there is no need for you any more, Brave Eagle. These ideas you fill her head with from books, they are all like clouds in the sky. You cannot touch them. They are not on the earth. She is mine, Brave Eagle. She does not need you and do not come by again."

Brave Eagle never liked Flat Iron, a brash young man, but this time his anger made the veins in his neck protrude. He fought the impulse to strike Flat Iron, but turned his back and walked away.

When Brave Eagle returned to his tipi, he sat in the dirt and Bone came over and licked his face.

"At least, I still have you to keep me company, Bone." Shaded Feather slept in the tipi. In fact, she slept most of the time. Brave Eagle awoke at sunrise and no matter what the weather, he and Bone found an isolated place where they watched the sun emerge. As the mood struck him, he might break into a sprint. Once, in freezing cold, he took off all his clothes and extended his arms to the sun. He remembered the Sun Dance ceremony in which barbed sticks were impaled into his chest and yanked out as a test of endurance. Every time he thought about that ceremony, his eyes welled with tears, for it hurt beyond any pain he ever felt, but only for a short while, and the trick was not to cry out in pain.

If it was to be the sun, or Jesus, or his books, Brave Eagle sought deliverance of some kind, but he did not know what. The ghost dance was an exercise in futility. The mere fact Flat Iron was one of its strongest advocates confirmed it. Yet, he danced with the rest of them, for like Onashola, he wondered, what if Wovoka was right? He hoped for another visit from Jesus, but this time he wanted to talk to the man, not hold his hand.

Sitting Bull, the medicine man, a Hunkpapa Sioux, another tribe's chief, was killed in much the same way as Crazy Horse, while resisting arrest. He cautioned to the tribe that he had been to the East and seen so many white people that they are coming and nothing can stop them. He was arrested to help thwart the Ghost Dance movement. News of his killing spread throughout the Sioux nation. It was only two weeks before Wounded Knee.

Sitting Bull's life and death represented the plight of the red man from the mid-19th century until the end. He was a noble warrior, a medicine man, and a leader of his people. When starvation threatened his tribe, he surrendered to the soldiers and was hired to be an attraction at Buffalo Bill's Wild West Show, where they re-enacted Little Big Horn. He returned to the tribe, and as the Ghost Dance emerged in popularity, his importance as a Sioux leader and the word he was involved in the movement led to his arrest and death. Brave Eagle was not close to Sitting Bull and did not join his expedition to Canada.

To seek out something to read, he missed Wounded Knee and his new life began. For the first time, he found love. For the first time, he brought children into the world.

George Pettigrew purchased a plot of land in the hills of South Dakota to mine for gold. He and his bride, Betty, moved from Massachusetts in 1872 and built the mansion, a farm and a smaller house down the road from Rapid City.

He spent a month learning everything he could about mining, working in a mine in Southern Illinois. Then, he was off to South Dakota with his bride, Betty. He hired an assistant, Eddy, and together they mined for almost a year before their find. They took what George calculated was enough to last two lifetimes. He gave Eddy ten percent, his share and they dynamited and sealed the mine. After selling the gold, he treated Betty to a weeklong vacation in San Francisco, where he opened an account and left some additional cash, some documents and the map to his mine. There was more to be mined, but the mining exhausted him and he envisioned a sedate future, enjoying the fruits of his labor, sitting on a front porch, idling the time away while Betty ran the library.

George and Betty were originally from Concord, Massachusetts and met in 1861. She was only nine years old, and George nineteen. George was in a wealthy family that owned several Concord businesses and Betty the daughter of a blacksmith who shod the heels of the horses of the wealthy.

George went off to the Civil War, where, in a twist of fate, he served under George Armstrong Custer. He was wounded only once, a superficial shoulder wound, and a miraculous accomplishment after some of the battles.

George found Custer to be daring reckless, but always had a knack for taking the initiative that left the Confederates at a loss. After hearing of Custer's demise at Little Big Horn, George told his wife, "Sounds like his risk-taking caught up with him."

Betty found it ironic when she learned from Brave Eagle that he killed Custer, the man her husband fought for in the Civil War.

After the war, George returned to Concord and in the ensuing years Betty grew into a beautiful young lady. She was 20 when they married, and George 29. George expanded the family business and cashed investments allowed him the luxury to go west. They first moved to Chicago where he continued his business successes. As a boy, he had visions of rushing out to the California gold rush, finding a fortune and relaxing the rest of his life, and the vision stayed with him. He chose South Dakota from words of new riches in the hills. His intention was to mine for a couple of years. If it did not work out, he would return with Betty to Chicago or Massachusetts. But if it did, they would settle in and try to raise a family.

The word of George's rich strike was the kiss of death. For adjacent to the land George prospected was land owned by Leo McEver. McEver made a fortune in the California gold rush. Born into a wealthy family, he set out with his two brothers to mine for gold and they succeeded and he was only nineteen years old. He proceeded to do a good job spending the money on whores. When the word came out about Dakota gold, he recognized a second opportunity, and moved only a week after George Pettigrew. He purchased a lot of land, built a hotel and a saloon and a dry goods store in Rapid City and the large ranch outside of town.

Leo McEver had no friends. Not even his brothers liked him. He attended a private school in Boston and been dismissed for threatening a teacher. Leo paid another boy to write an assignment for him, resulting in a mark of "F" and a handwritten letter to Leo's parents.

"I'm not going to give this to them," he told the teacher, a young man graduated from Harvard.

"I will," the teacher replied.

"You do and you'll never see another day!" the irate boy blurted, his face contorting with anger.

The teacher was so aghast at the reaction, he consulted with the principle and Leo's parents were summoned. It did not matter that they paid a healthy donation to the school. Leo was out. The teacher was hit from behind by a board and knocked unconscious while returning from school, one week after Leo's dismissal.

Leo's family was interrogated at length. They shipped Leo off to a boarding school, and he lasted three months before expulsion. He and two other boys assaulted a local ten-year old girl, holding her down while violating her with a ruler. Leo hated girls. They didn't like him, either. A whore in San Francisco told him, "You ain't good looking at all, but if you can pay, sure, why not?' and he proceeded to strangle her almost to unconsciousness. That got him a jail cell his brothers bailed him out of.

His first wife was a whore. She was the first woman that didn't complain he was rough and uncouth in his ways of amore. His sexual peccadillo was voyeurism. He paid men to have sex with his wife while he watched and he encouraged his wife to call him vile names during the act. "You ugly bastard. Look what I am doing in front of you!' That thrilled him all the more.

The first marriage lasted nine months when he caught the girl stealing his money in preparation to flee with another man. Two broken arms and a one thousand dollar sendoff sent her packing.

Another marriage a year later ended the same way. He continued in his pattern of finding a woman willing to have sex with others in his presence. Every once in a while he would join them. This woman left him when he shot her dog for peeing on the rug. He remained a wealthy bachelor, deciding it was easier to pay whores when the urge came over him.

He left San Francisco for South Dakota because he felt like a small man in a big city and wanted to find a place where he could be the big man in town. Rapid City was perfect. He quickly opened a hotel and saloon while funding his mining operation. He was the wealthiest man in town. With a payroll of twenty-five, he figured he had enough funds to mine most of South Dakota and dredge the earth.

He found his third wife in San Francisco, fifty years his junior but willing to make the move to the Dakotas as long as it included frequent trips back home and a lifetime stipend.

His mines in South Dakota came up empty and when he learned somewhere close by one of his neighbors made a big hit, and approached George Pettigrew about buying his property. They met at his saloon.

This meeting was in the early 1870s. McEver had been a heavy drinker, but stomach ulcers forced him to quit. Ironically, McEver was also from Massachusetts - his parents had left Ireland first for Boston, where his father owned a saloon catering to the Irish immigrants. McEver was the youngest of three children, but a rebellious child who had flattened his father in an argument with one punch at the age of 16. That is about when he left for the California gold rush with his two brothers.

"So, they tell me you hit big," McEver opened, sitting with his back to the saloon door opened to the street. He sat so George faced the window, where the glaring sun shone right into his eyes. George shifted his chair to deflect the light.

"Big enough." George expected this would bring an offer to purchase the land, but he had no intention.

"How much you pay for the land?"

"Two dollars an acre."

"I'll give you ten. What do you have? Twenty acres?"

"Fifteen and I ain't selling."

McEver leaned back in his chair and held his large belt buckle against his belly. "But I understand you've given up mining. What will you do with the land?"

"Donate to the Sioux."

"Why?"

"It's theirs. I got enough, sealed it up."

" Do you think you owe them anything? They'd as soon scalp you and rape your wife."

"You ever mine with your hands?"

"I did. In California. Didn't have to here."

"Didn't you feel something about the earth, the dirt?"

"It was in the way of gold, if that is what you mean."

" "You probably will never understand me. But, I ain't selling. I don't want it disturbed any more. I'd rather buy your land. How much do you want?"

"Leo McEver is not the one who does the selling!" McEver sputtered, his face reddening with anger. "Who do you think you are? Some librarian book loving, Indian lover?"

George cocked his head. "You don't know who you are talking to, do you?"

McEver spat, "A do-gooding Indian lover. There are a lot like you, feeling this is the Indians land. Yet you went in and pulled out enough gold that could house an entire tribe for a year."

George nodded, "I am aware of the fact. I am not greedy, like you. There are limits to a man's needs. I do not intend to be some Andrew Carnegie of the west."

"What's wrong with Carnegie?"

"There comes a point where there is too much and you give back. He could feed all the starving in Pennsylvania and still be a millionaire. He may be called a Philanthropist, sure."

"You should have stayed where you were, Concord, right? The Dakotas are wide open, the last frontier. People are afraid to move here. "

"So, let's come to this. I do not intend to sell the land. I am giving mine back. If you want to sell me yours, I will buy and give it back, too."

"We've talked enough. You are a fool, that's all I can say," McEver said.

George shrugged and left. McEver's men, who idled away at he bar while discussions ensued, prepared to leave.

"Joe, come here," McEver said to them.

Joe, one of his cowhands, came over and McEver pulled the chair.

"See that man?"

"Yeah."

"See he has an accident of some kind. Soon."

"How?"

"You figure a way."

"And when it's done, tell me. There will be a big payday for you. Big enough for you to leave this ranch and go buy your own."

George and Betty Pettigrew had a four-year old son, Will, and a determination to stay in Rapid City, South Dakota and continue to build their family. The night before the tragedy, George and Betty outlined the way they would spend their days in the town.

"What are you going to do now, George? We have enough now to last two lifetimes. I have the lending library. What are you going to do with yourself?"

"I'm going to help Will with his lessons. Maybe improve the schoolhouse. I'd like for him to get an education like yours. I quit when I was twelve. Who'd ever thought I'd marry a college graduate?"

"We could start a college here when he is old enough? I'd love for Will to get the kind of education you can get in the East. Make another Emerson out of him," Betty agreed.

Supper at the Pettigrew home featured cornbread; beans and beef doused in syrup and George stirred his biscuits in the syrup.

"A Dakota Harvard? It'd be nice to educate these Indians. They deserve it."

"They can probably teach us."

"That's certain. They don't appear to have greed like our neighbor McEver."

Betty was with child, seven months along with what would become Mathilda, a child that would die the day she was born. Perhaps the tragedy affected Betty's ability to bring Mathilda into the world.

That evening, George took Will for a walk, their summer custom. They walked not a hundred yards from the home when a rider on horseback approached from the town's direction. George moved Will to the side of the road to let the rider pass.

The horse veered, and appeared to be bearing down on them with the intention of running them over. Again, George moved off the road and as the horse slowed, George exclaimed "What's wrong with you?" and a man whose face was covered with a red kerchief aimed his pistol and shot twice. The horse reared and shrieked at the gunshots and brought its hooves down, trampling young Will. The man controlled the horse and left George and his son on the ground.

Betty was in the barn checking on their two cows, when the shots rang out, and she heard the shriek of the horse. She ran to the road, in the direction of the shots, and found George, his life draining from him, and nearby, Will, crushed. Up the road, a rider galloped away and she detected a red shirt and a hat. The only thing in that direction was the McEver ranch and beyond, miles of plains.

George was ashen, lying in a pool of blood, and gasped, "Will!" and Betty walked to the rumpled, lifeless body of her son, his head indented with a horse's hoof print. She placed her finger on Will's neck to detect a pulse, found none, and collapsed over his body, crying out, "Oh, Will! Will! No!" By the time she turned to her husband, he too was dead, his eyes staring at the heavens.

In one instant, her life changed from one of promises of a bright future to emptiness. Within minutes, several townspeople gathered at the sound of gunfire. Betty, ever the stoic, was inconsolable.

Four days later, Betty's mother and sister arrived from Massachusetts. George, an only child, had no family. After the funerals, her mother and sister tried to reason with her in the family living room. A family portrait hung over the mantle on the fireplace, giving Betty a constant reminder of her loss. Her mother, Constance, in her sixties, was prim and trim, dressed in Eastern finery; her gray hair swirled into a bun. Betty's lookalike sister Rebecca, a spinster of forty, also a librarian, held her sister's hand.

"Come back with us, Betty. You have no reason to stay in this God-forsaken place," Constance insisted.

"We can combine libraries in Concord, Betty. You have a good collection," Rebecca offered.

"I'm not ready to leave here. No. Dakota was our destiny. And if I were to leave, destiny would be unfulfilled."

"But how are you going to raise this child? You can't by yourself!" Constance argued. "Come home. I would like to see my grandchild grow up. George left you this child in your womb."

"Mother. Don't. I will come to visit. But George and Will are here and I am not going to leave them behind."

After Mathilda died at birth, Betty did not get out of bed for two weeks, sunk in deep depression. It was months before she woke one day, walked the quarter mile down the dirt road to the library and opened its doors. This was three years before Wounded Knee and eighteen months before Brave Eagle discovered the library for the first time. The man who murdered George and Will was never caught. The sheriff visited McEver the day after the murders, escorted by his deputy.

They were brought into his office, where McEver sat behind a huge presidential desk, his boots propped up on an ottoman. The room was a vivid shade of red, like you would expect in a brothel, with red drapes covering the windows behind the desk. A large painting of McEver with his two hounds drew their attention, above the mantel of a fireplace crackled logs despite the heat outside.

"Mr. McEver, a man was shot down the road, George Pettigrew, and his son killed. The killer was headed in your direction. He wore a red shirt. There's a good possibility it was one of your ranch hands."

"And he was wearing a red shirt? It narrows the possibilities. What time?"

"Before sunset. About eight or so. Mind if I ask some of your men?"

"Go ahead. The men live in the dormer out back. They're all in the field today, so you'll have to come back this evening."

"Fine. We'll be back after six."

After the sheriff and deputy left, McEver turned to his assistant, Jenkins.

"Too bad about the boy. Farrell's gone?"

"I put him on the stage. We'll never see him again."

"So we'll keep looking. He can't cover up a spot without some sort of marker. There is a map somewhere."

At the time, McEver employed twenty-five in his mining operations, a dozen cowhands who worked on the ranch, plus the staff of his Rapid City businesses. He had built a dormitory on his ranch to house the employees, but grew tired of having to bail two or three out every weekend when they went into Rapid City and caused a drunken ruckus.

His businesses began to erode. His men searched for George's site, and opened mines in land Betty Pettigrew owned, to no avail. Finally, he was down to five miners and only four cowhands. Jenkins, his assistant showed in 1905, he lost sixty thousand dollars. It was time to accelerate their efforts to find gold. Out of frustration, he ordered his men to rough up Mrs. McEver and search her house.

He called two men into his office. Jenkins sat across the room as the men stood awkwardly in front of their boss. These were roughnecks who had numerous jail terms, but McEver always kept a few like them on the payroll whenever he needed something unpleasant done.

"Here's what I want, men," McEver began, kicking his boots up on the ottoman. "The lady has some map or documents her husband left that can lead us to the location of the gold mine. I want you to go in, if she's home, tie her up or something. Do not harm her! Search the house for papers, maps. Bring them back to me and I will pay you well. But here is the catch. You don't work for me if you get caught or something goes wrong. I will help you get out of here and pay you when you deliver something of value to me and I am certain there is something. Look for a safe in the house. Check all the drawers. She's a harmless woman, but she may have a gun. And don't do it during the week when she has helpers in her house. No noise, either. Next door is that Indian. You don't want to disturb him again. Got it?"

"How much for us?" one of the men asked.

"Fifty in advance. But five hundred if you deliver what I am looking for."

"What ARE you looking for?"

"Maps. Mining notes. Things like that."

"We'll take care of it."

The men left and Jenkins commented, "And if we find nothing?"

"Time to give up mining. No one's coming up with gold any more.

His new wife, Carrie, one he found in a San Francisco store, knocked on the door.

"Come in."

"Honey, I'm bored."

"Come sit on my lap. That will be all, Jenkins."

Jenkins left, smiling leeringly at the blonde bombshell of a woman.

"Nothing to do here. When can we go back to California?"

"We'll go at the end of the summer. You won't like the winters here."

"All I do is watch the cowboys watching me. I think they would eat me if they could."

"You're right. They're not used to women like you and you don't discourage them looking at you. "

"I can't stay inside all day. And I don't like riding horses, either. It hurts my place."

"I can imagine. And I don't want that place to be sore," he put his hand between her thighs."

"That's the ticket. Can we go to the bedroom for a while without Jenkins interrupting you all the time?" Anything special in mind this time?"

"I like the ropes and blindfold."

"Business can wait!"

CHAPTER 4

BRAVE EAGLE AND Onashola raised their daughters in the same skills they perfected: archery, hunting, running, and shooting. They travelled to the South Dakota state fair, where Maka, now 14, and Wishiwu, 12, earned blue ribbons in every athletic event they tried. They attended a two-room schoolhouse. There were only forty students from the ages of six to sixteen, so the classes divided into four groups: six to eight year-olds, nine to eleven, twelve to fourteen and fifteen and sixteen. Still, it was more of a formal education than their parents received. The two girls plowed through the library as if the building was about to close.

Baseball was popular in South Dakota and Maka discovered a talent for hurling the ball with great speed. Word of mouth spread about a teen-aged girl who struck all the boys out, and one day the manager of the amateur Rapid City team asked her to pitch to his team in an exhibition game. She pitched to nine players, striking seven of them out. One hit a feeble dribbler to the second baseman. Rapid City's best player did connect on a solid line drive to the outfield, so the manager asked Brave Eagle if Maka could join the team. Brave Eagle refused to let his daughter play, however. The team barnstormed to other towns in the Dakotas and Nebraska, and he did not want his daughter's education interrupted, much less travel with tobacco-chewing, profanity-laden players.

Brave Eagle figured he was in his sixties somewhere, and Onashola in her late thirties. He was still in good health, and had out-lived many of the men of his generation in the Lakota tribe. Sixty was considered an old man, although he still possessed superior strength. One indication of slowing down: for the first time Onashola bested him in a foot race. They marked off a line in front of their house and ran down the dirt road about a mile to a line in front of a neighbor's house. In 1906, for the first time, Onashola surged ahead of Brave Eagle, but only because she tried to stay ahead of Maka and Wishiwu, who nipped at her heels.

"Don't slow down for my sake," Brave Eagle panted, and Maka passed her mother, pushed to the limit by Wishiwu.

Brave Eagle pulled out his pocket watch. "Under seven minutes. And the three of you under six minutes."

Onashola held her husband's hand. She knew she could beat Brave Eagle for some time, but competing with her daughters inspired her to stay ahead of them, and she felt bad they all finished so far ahead of her husband.

"You have been holding back, fine. I am not as fast as I used to be," Brave Eagle said. "But, if I had to, I could run to Omaha."

"So could I," Maka laughed. Maka surpassed her mother's height, about five-five. As they grew, the two sisters were mistaken for twins, with lustrous black hair. Wishiwu braided her hair into two long ponytails, to help the locals tell them apart. "Two tailed girl" was her nickname.

A number of Native American settled into Rapid City, mostly Lakota and Cheyenne. The majority of the Sioux settled into the Pine Ridge Reservation. The Indian wars were over. They had been overrun. Utah was the forty-fifth state admitted to the Union, in 1896. Oklahoma soon became the forty-sixth state.

Only eight years before, the United States fought the Spanish-American war, a fight for Cuban independence. The war lasted only ten weeks and resulted in a US victory. Theodore Roosevelt was president.

And in 1906 the world of Brave Eagle and Onashola fell apart. An idyllic existence, watching their beautiful and strong daughters grow into young replicas of their mother, turned into chaos.

South Dakota was in the midst of a long winter. Winters tended to last five months; with a short spring before a long summer and a short fall. On Saturdays, Betty Pettigrew took the day off, while Brave Eagle managed the library. He was the assistant librarian now, rather than a book filer.

On those mornings, Maka and Wachiwi stayed at the Pettigrew house while Onashola went to the town markets. Betty employed a Swedish woman, Ingrid, as a cook and housekeeper, as the German couple moved to Minnesota.

After Brave Eagle and Onashola left their daughters with Mrs. Pettigrew, a wagon stopped in front of the house. Two men vaulted from the carriage and burst into the house.

Ingrid carried a tray from the kitchen and turned into the dining room. The men startled her and she dropped the tray to the ground. They pointed their six-shooters. One of the men, a red-haired freckled face man, put his finger to his mouth. He wore his hat tilted back, and dusty jeans with a buffalo skin, fringed jacket.

"Quiet. Over there." He motioned with his pistol. "Take her."

The other man, a bearded cowboy with a droopy right eye, roughly covered Ingrid's mouth, and pushed her into a chair by a kitchen table. He came prepared, stuffing a kerchief into her mouth and tying her to the chair.

"Ingrid?" Betty Pettigrew called from the dining room.

Mrs. Pettigrew sat at the head of the table. Maka and Wishiwu sat on either side, reading. Plates were set out in front of them, as they awaited Ingrid to deliver breakfast.

"What is this?"

"I'll tell you what it is. Stay where you are. Don't move. We didn't come to hurt you but will if you don't tell us what we want to know."

"What is that?"

"We want the map. Your husband had a map. You know where it is."

"I don't know anything about a map."

The other cowboy came into the room.

"Tie them up, Joseph."

They pointed their pistols at Mrs. Pettigrew and the girls. Maka looked across the table at Wishiwu. "How do we escape?" and scanned the room.

Joseph tied Maka and Wishiwu, gagging their mouths with kerchiefs, then Betty Pettigrew.

"Now. Where is the safe and what is the combination? Don't waste our time."

Mrs. Pettigrew shook her head and stayed tight-lipped, and the freckled cowboy struck her across the cheek with his gun, opening a wide, bloody gash.

"Where?"

"It is in my nightstand. Right 34, left 6, right 18."

"Got it. Watch em!"

"All right, Andy."

A few minutes later, Cowboy Andy, the freckled man, returned with a bag of money and an envelope.

"Looks like we are going to the bank for a withdrawal, Joseph. In San Francisco. I'm going to search the house."

For thirty minutes the man moved furniture, searched beneath beds, and in closets. He returned with a pillowcase full of a jewel box and papers.

"We're taking the girls with us to be sure, Miss. If the map is not in the safe deposit box in the bank, we're going to keep them until you tell us where the map is. So do you want to tell us before we go to all the trouble?"

"It might be in the bank. It might not. "

"We think different."

Joseph loosened the ropes around each girl and pushed them both. "Go ahead, little missies. We won't hurt you. Yet."

Andy gagged Mrs. Pettigrew and gave one final twist of the rope to make sure it was tied extra tight around the chair. As they walked through the house, they saw Ingrid fallen to the floor in her chair, still tied. She looked up as they walked the girls out of the house.

"Sorry, Swede," Joseph exclaimed as he left.

They shoved the girls into the back of a covered wagon. Wishiwu sat next to some pruning shears and though her hands were tied behind her back, she positioned them between her hands.

"It wasn't the plan to take the girls," Joseph said.

"No, but I figure she's going to pay up for them. After we get the map, and those papers McEver wants, we give her an ultimatum, maybe a thousand more dollars for the girls."

"But McEver only wants the map. We can't bring these girls to the ranch."

"This will be our own money. The five hundred he's giving us is not enough. I figure when we get the map, we ask for even more from him," Andy said.

"Oh, I don't want to mess with him. A few ranch hands vanished when they disagreed with him. Pulling a fast one over him doesn't seem like a good idea."

"If we work it right. He doesn't know about these girls."

"But their father. He's the one cut your ankles."

"And this is where I get my revenge."

"You're not thinking of killing them?"

"I'm thinking I don't know what I'm thinking.'"

"You won't believe what I found in the box!"

He opened the bag and showed a stack of money.

"Must be ten thousand dollars in here!"

"Is the map?"

"No. But I found another key to the First Bank of San Francisco I bet it's there. Looks like we are going to California!"

"We could take the money and not tell him about the key," Joseph said.

"Our days in South Dakota ended. The way I see it, we get the map, come back and sell it to him."

"Where we going?'

"Omaha. That's where we're gonna get on the train. But first, there's an old whore I want to spend some money on."

"But what about the girls? "

"Leave em somewhere, I don't know. I'm making this up as we go along. Throw them off the train?"

At about the same time as Andy and Joseph aimed their carriage to Omaha, Onashola arrived at the Pettigrew home. She opened the door and found Ingrid lying on the floor, tied to the chair and gagged. She removed the gag around her mouth.

"What happened? Where are Maka and Wishiwu?"

"Two men came. They tied us up and took the girls. They beat Mrs. Pettigrew!"

Onashola untied Ingrid and sprinted to the dining room where she found Mrs. Pettigrew, her face bleeding, a wide gash across her cheek. Her eyes puffed with tears.

"Where are they?" Onashola asked.

"They took them I think they're going to my San Francisco bank!"

Onashola ran out to the stable and mounted a horse, while Mrs. Pettigrew hitched a horse to the wagon. "They will either take the money and run or go to California."

"Is this all the money?"

"No. I have money in accounts, and that was not the only key. They were after my husband's map in San Francisco, with some more money."

"I'll get Brave Eagle."

Onashola rode to the library and found Brave Eagle at the front desk, reading a newspaper.

"Two men took our girls! They robbed Mrs. Pettigrew and rode away with our girls."

"Which way did they go?"

"They got her safe deposit box and she thinks they went to San Francisco. They were after a map of Mr. Pettigrew's gold mine."

"They would go to Omaha and take the train. Did she describe the men to you?"

"A red haired man and a bearded man with drooped eyes."

"That's the cowboy who works for McEver at his ranch. The man I cut his ankles. He was still around."

Onashola and Mrs. Pettigrew reported to the Sheriff and went to the McEver ranch to make sure the men had not gone there.

Brave Eagle, after feeding and watering his horse, packed his saddle-bags and took the road east that would pass through Sioux Falls and Sioux City on the way to Omaha. As the first westbound wagon approached, he inquired if they saw a covered wagon going east driven by two cowboys. He was one or two hours behind them. He estimated he could overtake them sometime in the second day. However, he did not anticipate the men took a detour to Pierre, and he continued east, off their trail.

Sheriff Jameson, who was new in town, took one of his Deputies, Deputy Bjorkman along with Betty Pettigrew and Onashola to the McEver Ranch. McEver employed about eight cowhands and an assistant.

His ranch was situated on over 5000 acres and included a dormitory for his hired hands. He owned about fifty horses and a couple hundred sheep.

Betty Pettigrew always knew McEver had something to do with her husband's murder. Either he hired someone, or one of his men did it. All it took was to mention something to two or three people and over time, to make the whole of Rapid City aware the reason the Pettigrews were wealthy. McEver could not get enough.

Sheriff Jameson, Betty and Onashola entered the main room of the ranch, the size of a hotel lobby, with a bison's head framed above a giant fireplace over eight feet tall. It was too hot for a fire, though, as the windows opened for ventilation. A servant directed them to a setting of four brown leather sofas huddled in a square in the center of the room.

McEver's aide, Jenkins, sat before McEver walked in, carrying a Persian cat. His wife Carrie walked with him. Carrie kissed McEver, a weathered-looking seventy year old with a deeply tanned face. He walked with a cane, leaning to one side, and sat across from the others.

"Sheriff, do what do I owe the pleasure and who are these ladies?"

"Mr. McEver, this is Betty Pettigrew and Onashola Heard. Mrs. Pettigrew was robbed this morning by two men who everyone says worked for you, and they took Mrs. Heard here's daughters as hostages."

"Who are these men you say work for me?"

"One is a red headed man named Andy and the other is a bearded man named Joseph with a bad eye."

McEver snorted and looked at his aide. "Andy Jones and Joseph Mathias. They did work for me but they did not show up today and I wondered."

"They wanted a map," the Sheriff continued. "They thought the late Mr. Pettigrew had a map where he discovered gold in the Black Hills."

"Oh. Well, they served time in prison before I hired them, and I thought they reformed. Did they get the map, Mrs. Pettigrew?"

"What they got were Onashola's daughters and some money. They said they were headed to San Francisco to my bank and see if the map is in a box there."

"What bank?"

"The First Bank."

McEver stared at Onashola with such intensity she felt him undressing her with his eyes. She looked away and could not meet his stare.

"I'll be doing that."

"They will stop through Sioux Falls. You can alert the sheriff."

"Done."

"So, Sheriff, all I can say is I had nothing to do with this. They acted on their own. I am sorry, ladies. I hope your daughters are safe and they are caught."

"If those men come back here, I want you to let me know," Jameson said.

"I will. Is that all?" he pulled himself into a standing position with his cane and nodded. Rodney, will you show our guests out?"

The servant led the entourage out of the room. McEver turned to his assistant, Jenkins. "Find those asses! Send some men after them and find them before Brave Eagle does."

Long trips on dirt roads had its share of dangers. Stage coaches traveled daily through South Dakota to Rapid City', but road traffic was limited to a few voyagers moving west or east as the case may be. Hours could go by without seeing another traveler. There was the threat of bandits around every curve.

Brave Eagle stayed aware. His hand was on his pistol whenever he came to a bend in the road or a hilly throughway. Several horsemen cut across a side trail ahead of him. As he neared a blind bend, a lone rider appeared on the crest of the hill to his right. He pulled his horse off the road under the cover of some bushes. This was a bandit, not an Indian.

A deer trail led to the ridge, and he got off his horse. Hoof prints in the dirt showed the way the rider had taken. He considered riding a wide path and returning to the road far up ahead, but that would add hours to his journey.

The man was about three hundred yards up the trail; so Brave Eagle tied his horse to a tree and stealthily made his way up the trail. Only a bandit in a den of robbers would take the trail to that precise position. This was an ambush.

Brave Eagle made his way to within a few feet of the rider, who sat looking down over the road. The man was exposed to the sun and his shirt soaked in sweat and the man's body odor was so repugnant, Brave Eagle recoiled. He leapt, grabbing the man's shirt at the collar and pulling him backwards to the ground. He punched the man once, hard to the side of the head, and the blow knocked the man unconscious, but the horse bolted, neighed, and rode away, down the hill to the other side. That would alert the others.

The man was about thirty years old, with a scruffy mustache and no beard. Brave Eagle suspected another one of McEver's ranch hands. He undid the man's holster and took his six-shooter before returning to his own horse. Now, his options were to follow the same trail, or go back to the road, or perhaps find a trail on the opposite side of the road.

When he retrieved his horse, he saw five of them, galloping down the road. He put the bandit's holster around his waist and pulled out his own pistol, and lay his rifle on the ground. He sank to the ground, into the dirt and almost tasted the soil. He prepared for an endless wait. The men broke up to search the area, and two of them got off their horses and walked straight in his direction.

Brave Eagle took aim and shot the man on the left in the heart and the one on the right, reaching for his gun, through the side of his face. He collapsed to the ground, screaming, but not dead. Brave Eagle grabbed the reins of his horse, and started back up the deer trail. He heard riders behind him, following, shouting, "There he goes!" But his horse, Light Foot lived up to her name, she was fast up the trail and passed the unconscious bandit, and headed down the trail on a steep decline towards the road.

The downward trail was tricky to negotiate, with loose rocks, and Light Foot slid, and failing to gain footing, fell, and with Brave Eagle still on, hit the dirt and slid on her side, but righted herself and regained her footing. Somehow and despite having the horse slide, Brave Eagle only suffered abrasions on his arms and legs. But Light Foot seemed to gather her senses when she stood, and at that moment in clear sight of the outlaws at the top of the hill, shots rang out. Light Foot was hit by two bullets and toppled over. Brave Eagle jumped to the cover of his own horse as the bullets rained down and looked straight into his horse's eyes, full of pain. He shot Light Foot in the head to put her out of her misery.

Five cowboys to battle, one wounded and another unconscious, but not for much longer. He carried his saddlebags. He had food and water, and $700 inside, and two horses available if he caught them before the men shot him. So, he turned and ran. At the sight of him on the run, two horsemen made their way down the hill, struggling to maintain balance, and both of them met the same fate as Light Foot, tumbling over in the loose rocks. One of the men, crushed by his own horse, and cried out in agony, as the other managed to climb back on his horse and proceed down the trail.

Brave Eagle moved fast and emerged to the road. But when he stepped out to the road, two cowboys saw him from a quarter mile away and spurred into a gallop. Brave Eagle stood in the middle of the road, raised his arms to the sky and from deep in his chest yelled a primeval Sioux war cry, "YEYYYAA!" One of the riders pulled on his reins at the sound and stopped his horse. He knew the sound and wanted no part of it, but the other cowboy, his face bleeding, charged on.

"Let him come to his death," Brave Eagle thought. The man aimed a rifle from his horse while in full gallop and Brave Eagle pointed his gun, waited until the man was within range, and blasted him off the horse. The horse continued to run past Brave Eagle, so he gave chase until the horse stopped. Brave Eagle vaulted into the saddle, still carrying his saddle bags, and rode away. He glanced back, and another rider came off the trail, but did not give chase.

After a while, Brave Eagle figured the men did not follow. He found a creek where he watered the horse, undressed and soaked in the water. He had a big scratch along his leg, his knees and arms bled. But not bad, considering the damage done to the posse of men. It was to be a long journey.

He lay back on the creek bank, needing rest. He thought back to the moment of Maka's birth, when the midwife handed their new baby for him to hold, as Onashola looked on weary from labor.

"Hello, my tiny girl!" he said and Maka looked him straight in the eye like she knew him. She listened to his voice from the womb. It was a look of fondness and recognition. I know you. What to do with her? He knew nothing about the care of babies, but Onashola was caring and protective. She would not let anything happen to this one. The first year, she awoke for feedings several times in the night, and though Onashola cared for her, Brave Eagle woke every time, tired and fatigued throughout the day. Why could I not be twenty years younger? He bolstered his own determination. "I am Brave Eagle. I do not tire. I do not give in to fatigue."

They progressed through her development, watching with excitement as she took her first steps and began to speak. She took an immediate interest in books, as her parents seemed engrossed in one at all times, so did she want to know what was behind those covers. Then the news came Onashola was with child again. A second miracle.

Wishiwu came into the world two years after her sister, Maka. She seemed to be born a jokester full of heyoka. She did not gravitate to books like her family, but was lured by Mrs. Pettigrew's piano. Whenever Betty Pettigrew sat down to play, little Wishiwu shook her little butt and smiled.

Maka was very jealous of Wishiwu at first, having to share the attention of her parents.

When Maka ran, Brave Eagle saw a young Onashola. She ran with all the grace and swiftness of her mother. Few girls even bothered to run, when their mothers considered it unladylike. Not so Maka. If not for her sister Maka, Wishiwu was the fastest little girl runner in the town. Both little girls outran even the teenaged boys by the time they were ten and eight. The boys had a simple understanding at the school, "It is a mistake to try to impress the Heard girls."

Brave Eagle would not let them get away. He only left Rapid City once for more than a couple of days, to go to Sioux Falls for some purchases for the library. Other than that, he had never been separated from his family. He intended to kill the two men that took them, pure and simple. If his daughters were harmed, the killing would not be clean; it would be slow and agonizing. Here is where he veered from what the church taught him about forgiveness. His intention was more of the Old Testament way, an eye for an eye. But if he caught up with those men, it would be more like an eye, a throat, and a head for an eye.

He wondered how any man could keep them subdued for any length of time. They were trained like Brave Eagle. Point a pistol at him, and he had five ways to evade harm. At Little Big Horn, he had the moment, when he rode his horse straight at Custer, and Custer looked him in the eye, cocked his pistol and fired, but the gun was out of bullets. He saw in Custer's eyes the awareness, he faced certain death. That was not the first time he charged at a gun and every time, they either missed or, in Custer's case, had no bullets. He taught his daughters to look an assailant in the eye, and use your feet. They knew a sidelong leap designed to drop a man to his knees and disarm them on the ground. They practiced it endlessly. All the tricks he taught them, and now they must use them.

After a brief rest, Brave Eagle started back. He stopped the first carriage, a family of a man, his wife and two grown sons, in a covered wagon.

"Bandits ahead, maybe an hour up the road," he warned.

"We have guns."

"You'll need them. There is a hill on the left and a woodsy area in the right. They are on both sides."

"How did you make it out?"

Brave Eagle shrugged. "And, did you see a wagon like yours going east with a red-haired man and a bearded man?"

"No, Been on the road all day and nary a rider or nuthin. You are the first we seen."

"Hmm. I'll go on, then. Be careful."

Brave Eagle began to wonder. Maybe they pulled off the road somewhere and he missed them. It was to be a very long trip, not knowing. The plan was to head for the Western Union office in Sioux Falls and Mrs. Pettigrew was to leave a message for him.

Betty Pettigrew soothed Onashola's rising anxiety, daily visiting the smaller house and sitting on the front porch, waiting.

"That man survived the Indian wars. He'll bring them back," she told her.

"I have every faith in him," Onashola responded. "And I pity the man who tries to harm my daughters. But finding them in a city is what concerns me."

"Thank God for the wire service. Brave Eagle can let us know when he gets to the train stations and I'll be leaving messages for him there. And after he finds them and brings them back, McEver will pay. It's his men he's putting up to this!"

"How much gold did your husband find?"

"By the time he sold it all, we had accumulated over one hundred fifty thousand dollars."

"My God!"

Betty marveled at the turns her life had taken, from a proper New England upbringing to a tough woman in the Wild West. She had lost Ingrid, her housekeeper, who moved on to Sioux City after the incident, leaving Betty alone in the mansion.

Mike was the only man she ever loved, from her teenaged years on. She weathered the murder of her husband and son and death of her daughter, yet still stuck it out to fulfill her husband's destiny, to make something out of his hands in the American West.

"Maybe it's wrong of me, sticking through this. But I've been wronged. You've been wronged. If there is an ounce of determination left in my body, it will be to find justice for me and for you. Enough is enough. I wish I had the powers of Brave Eagle and could take on these men all by myself. I think I would brand them with an iron!"

"We have our own ways."

"I hate Leo McEver. I never in my life could say I hated someone. But when I see that man, I see evil personified. Look at that nose of his. Somebody punched him so hard it's caved in. I'd like to drive it into his skull."

"He's a coward sending his bandits to do his dirty work. All for a piece of paper. And what is he supposed to do with the map? You still own the land."

"I've thought about the why of all this. He intends to open the mine back up. Nobody's out there, guarding the land. He expects to take what he can, close it up and say he got more gold from his own land."

Sheriff Raymond Jameson arrived as the two ladies conversed on the porch. Since the kidnappings, he made daily visits to Betty's house to check on her.

He was over sixty, a widower himself, and Rapid City was his third sheriff position, taking it on after stints in Kansas. He sported a white wide-brimmed Stetson hat creased down the middle, and doffed the hat as he approached. There was a gash across his face from a bullwhip a drunken cowboy slashed at him on the streets of Kansas City. He pursed his lips in thought and muttered, "Nothing yet. Just came over from the wire office."

"A good thing we can send those wires. It would help if we all had telephones," Betty remarked.

"Maybe some day. Another year and the trains will stop here and that ought to bring more telephones. For now, you send telegrams through Western Union."

Raymond had been a lawman for thirty-seven years, the first seven in Lawrence and the last thirty in Kansas City on the Kansas side. He kept a log of all his arrests and ultimate convictions. He witnessed seven of his arrests hang. Justice was usually well-served and swift in Kansas. Among his arrests was one woman who killed her husband because he complained about her cooking. There was a man who shot another man out of a tree and said he thought he was shooting a deer. He had come upon one gruesome murder in which the victim was dismembered and that unfortunately was an image that twenty years afterwards still haunted him.

His wife Mary Beth died the year before he retired from Kansas City. They rode back from a Sunday picnic in their carriage when she had a heart attack and was gone before he could reach the doctor. They had two grown sons who practiced law together in Kansas City. Jameson and Jameson. Mary Beth was really all he knew. He'd met her in his first year as sheriff when she worked in the dry goods store.

They envisioned a retirement away from Kansas and discussed Rapid City because her brother lived there and ran an auction practice. So, Raymond followed through on that promise when the job opened up in Rapid City and Bart Gray told him about it. He figured small town life meant drunken cowboys and the occasional shootout and he was right. What he didn't like was the lenient judge who was obviously in McEver's hip pocket considering the light sentences those men received.

He knew of the Pettigrew murder from his brother Bart, but in his second year as sheriff, this incident was his first real introduction to Betty Pettigrew. He knew her as the librarian but he had not once set foot in the library. He could read, all right, but had never read a book for pleasure. All he read were wanted posters and legal documents.

Rapid City had experienced lean times almost from the day he set foot in the town, where word of mouth was that the gold was all gone and half the population left. He had to drop one of his deputies because he couldn't afford to pay two.

"Missus Pettigrew, when is the library open?"

"Tuesday, Thursday, Friday and Saturdays from 10 to 4 in summer."

"So, how's it work? Do you have to pay?"

"Absolutely not. It's a lending library. I'll give a book for two weeks."

"What if it takes longer than two weeks to read?"

"You can renew it, unless someone else has requested the book."

"Where do you get all the books?"

"Some are donated. I go into Chicago twice a year for an order of new books."

"And how many do you have?"

"A few hundred. You should come in sometime. You must be able to read."

"Yes, but never read a book after school. You read, too, Miss Onashola?"

Onashola lifted a book from her lap and smiled.

"I know this must be a hard time for you to concentrate on anything other than your family, Miss."

Onashola nodded but did not speak, and looked off into the distance. Somewhere to the West, her husband journeyed in search of their daughters. There was a reason her destiny was intermingled with Brave Eagle's. She had every reason to believe he would come through on his quest.

CHAPTER 5

Joseph and Andy, McEver's roughnecks pulled their carriage down a back alley in Pierre. They wore field coats covering red cloth shirts covered in trail dust, with plain white kerchiefs wrapped around their necks and well worn crushed hats. It was sundown in early spring, and when the sun dropped, the temperature plummeted down to the twenties. The sounds of a honky tonk piano and raucous voices echoed out the back door of the local saloon where boisterous cowboys had the same idea have a few drinks and unwind. Those that could afford it would gravitate towards the local brothel.

"What do we do with these girls?"

Maka leaned in from the rear of the carriage to listen to the discussion, her mouth gagged, and soaked with saliva. Wishiwu showed free of the bonds.

"Let's go into the saloon and drink and get liquored up. We can trade this wagon for some fresh horses. They'll be looking for a wagon. Hell, I say we leave em here. They'll slow us down."

"They are the only protection we have. If they get away, we'd walk into that bank in California and they'd put the handcuffs on us. After we get that box out of the bank, I don't care what happens to them. How much money do we have?" Joseph asked.

"Over nine thousand. By now, McEver is probably sending some of the men looking for us."

"If we bring him the map he'll be happy, that's all he wants. But the more I think about it, we get the map, see what he will pay. Our days of working for him are over. We settle with him, split the money, you can go your way and I can go mine."

"Where will you go?"

"Arizona. I'm tired of freezing in South Dakota. You?"

"As far away from McEver as possible. He will hunt us down and kill us. I wouldn't trust him once his hands are on the map. Greedy bastard. Because he can't find any more gold in the hills, he still has enough money to last five lifetimes, and the woman of his, whew, wonder how much he paid for her. He's an ugly man, don't you think? She's a whore to sleep with a man as pig ugly as him. Ugh. No wonder, I think she takes opium so she can survive sexing up with that man. She has to imagine he is somebody else, cause he does look like a pig."

"If he's a pig, he's a smart pig. And you're right. We hand him the map and he shoots us. Here we are at the saloon."

Maka eased away from her sister, her hands still tied behind her back, and Wishiwu put her hands behind her back, clasping the rope.

Joseph and Andy pulled the wagon to the rear of the Pierre saloon. Pierre was another frontier town, about the same size as Rapid City, but to Joseph and Alfred's delight, it had more saloons and brothels. They climbed off the wagon and Joseph walked to the rear and peeked in. Wishiwu faced him so he could not see her free, untied hands.

"You girls need to piss or something?"

They shook their heads.

"We're going in here a while. So go to sleep, nighttime. And don't try to get out of here. Remember, you run from us and your parents will pay cause we have more men back in Rapid City. You run. They die. Simple as that."

As soon as they left, Wishiwu pulled the kerchief from her mouth, untied her sister's hands and removed her gag.

"Let's go."

"But they said...."

"No cowboy is gonna do anything to them. Can you imagine what would happen if they tried? Father could break them in two with his bare hands!"

They found themselves in the alleyway of a row of wooden buildings.

"Where are we?" Wishiwu asked.

"Didn't you hear? Pierre. Let's get away from here."

Pierre was arranged much like Rapid City and many western towns, in square blocks of neat rows of framed buildings. They walked several blocks until they saw a woman enter the back door of a two-story building. They followed her inside and came into a large kitchen, with overhanging pots and pans and a large table with fruits and meat and breads. Maka took a loaf of bread, tore it in half and handed half to her sister, grabbed two apples.

"Somebody here might help us."

They walked through the kitchen and climbed a wide, red-carpeted stairway, leading to a balcony. They leaned over, and on the first floor, saw men and women mingling. The women dressed scantily with blouses pulled low to display their breasts. One woman took a man by the hand and led him up the stairway, and Maka pointed to a closed door that led to a room and they scampered inside.

In the center of the room lay an old man in a bed, his mouth wide open, his eyes sunken and hollow.

With closed eyes, he asked, "Is that you, Mary?"

Maka motioned for them to go to another room and they looked to see if the hallway was clear, crossed the hallway and entered another room.

It was a bedroom with a canopy bed, a nightstand with a mirror on top, a wooden bath tub full of water and a porcelain pot.

"We're in a hotel," Maka said.

"Does the door lock?"

Maka tested the handle, "No."

Wishiwu opened a door. "It's a closet. And a blanket and a pillow in here."

"We can stay in this closet and if nobody comes, sleep in the bed tonight. Then we find the sheriff."

"What was wrong with that old man? He looked almost dead. I am so tired and sore from that wagon," Wishiwu said. She spread the blanket on the closet floor. "Only one pillow."

"I don't know. He was pretty sick, I think, there are two on the bed. I'll get one of those."

They closed the closet door and lay on the floor, lengthwise so their feet touched sole to sole. The blanket covered their legs. They fell asleep in minutes, but a couple hours later, a woman and a man came into the room, carrying lanterns for light. Maka stirred her sister and motioned for silence.

"Been a while, darling," the woman said.

"Had to save up some money," the man replied.

"Am I your teacher again?"

"Yes. The same."

Maka and Wishiwu sat up to listen to the people in the room.

"You are my best student."

"Thank you, ma'am. I try."

"You did well on those tests. As a reward, well, what do you want?"

"You know what I want."

"Do you want some more tutoring?"

"No, that's not it."

"What?"

"Your breasts."

"Oh! Why I don't know you've been that good."

Maka and Wishiwu glanced at each other and shrugged. Wishiwu was about to giggle and Maka motioned again for complete silence.

"I promise I will do even better on the next test," the man continued.

"If you promise. Put your hand in. Good."

"Can I suck them?"

"Yes, I think they need sucking."

The woman moaned softly.

"My, you are getting good at this."

The moaning intensified and her breathing labored.

"Where you want to go. Put your finger. There. There. You are my best student. You know what to do and let me. Oh, you are getting big now! Very, very big. It's time, boy."

The bedsprings began to creak.

Wishiwu whispered, "Let's see."

Maka opened the closet slightly, and saw a man's feet dug into the end of the bed so she pulled the door closed again and shrugged.

"I love you teacher," the man said.

"No other boys can do this. Harder!"

Maka grimaced and her sister held her hand to her mouth to keep from laughing.

The man let out a gasp, "There! You lowly whore! Take it all you evil bitch!"

"Oh, I am your evil bitch you bad, bad boy."

They got up and walked into the tub on the other side of the room. As she walked close to the closet, the woman said, "You been practicing, I can tell. That was the best yet. "

For a half hour, the couple chatted and the occasional splash of water, and Maka and Wishiwu lost interest and fell asleep. But, as the couple in the room dried off and prepared to leave the room, Maka rolled over in the closet and bumped her head on the wall.

"What was that?" the prostitute opened the closet doors.

"What are you doing here?" Maka groggily opened her eyes. She lay on the floor and Wishiwu did not stir, so she shook her sister with her feet.

"Sleeping."

"But what are you doing, sleeping in here? "

"We were hiding from some men."

The girls stood and the prostitute, who had a bushy head of blonde hair and despite the bath, heavily perfumed, with thick rouge on her cheeks, about twenty years old and tall and with a large chest her blouse, did little to cover.

"Stay right here. Don't move. Come on, Jerry, We'll go downstairs. I need to get Alice."

They left the room.

"Should we run?" Wishiwu asked.

"To where? It's night. Maybe the lady will let us sleep here until we find their sheriff."

The blonde prostitute returned with a middle-aged woman, whose perfume seemed to enter the room before she did. She had dark brown hair curled long down each side of her face, resembling the wigs English barristers wore in court, stout, and a few decades of drinking gave her alcoholic -tinged bags beneath her eyes.

"How did you get here, girls?"

"Through the back door. Two men captured us from our house in Rapid City and we escaped. We need to find the sheriff." Maka said.

The Madame looked the sisters up and down, from their heads to their feet, appraising them.

"What did these men look like?"

"Ugly," Wishiwu offered.

"A red-haired freckle-faced man named Andy and a bearded man named Joseph."

The Madame raised her eyebrows. "They are downstairs now. Two of our customers."

Wishiwu grabbed Maka's arm. "Don't let them find us! We want to go home!"

"You can stay here for the night and we will get the sheriff tomorrow," she paused. "How old are you?"

"I'm fourteen and Wishiwu is twelve," Maka said.

"And your name is?"

"Maka."

"I am Miss Alice and this is Miss Molly. So, go ahead, you can sleep in the bed instead of the floor."

As they left, and walked out of the room, down the stairs to the congregation of customers and prostitute, Molly said to Miss Alice, "They are pretty."

"They are. I know what you're thinking."

"I think the older one is as old as Britt."

"But Britt has those unbelievable boobs for a fourteen-year old."

"You could make a lot of money with them."

"I realize that. But I don't like employing anyone not sixteen. After all, they are still almost children."

"Didn't stop you with Britt."

"Well, she looks a lot older and she wanted to. She makes more money in one night than most of the girls make all week.'

"I see a gold mine with the older one, Miss Alice."

"We'll talk about it tomorrow."

The next morning, Miss Alice and Molly returned to the room. Maka and Wishiwu slept in the bed, and Miss Alice stirred them.

"Wake up, sleepy heads!"

Maka and Wishiwu awoke, taking the room in the light for the first time.

"Those men left, so it is safe to come out. The sheriff comes here often and is a friend of mine, so I will fetch him later today. You could use a bath. We'll put in some fresh water and get you some new clothes. You can come on down to the kitchen now and have some eggs for breakfast."

"Oh, good." Wishiwu said.

"We will write your parents and they come and get you. But in the meantime, you could serve the men drinks downstairs and I'll pay you something. Come on down and get something to eat. Those men are long gone."

The girls followed Miss Alice and Molly to breakfast. Later, the Sheriff came by to the brothel. Miss Alice talked with him.

"They are just delicious. If they get used to the life in the house, they won't want to return home. So, can we not be so fast about notifying the parents?"

"Let me see them myself, if they are as beautiful as you say."

"You will."

The girls sat on stools in the kitchen, devouring half of a chocolate cake.

"These are the girls from Rapid City," he said. He wore his Sheriff's badge over a leather vest and dingy linen shirt. He had a long, curly mustache twirled at each end, a masculine man, tall and rangy, and he carried his ten- gallon hat in large hands.

"Why don't you write down your parent's address for me and I will send a letter to them."

"Could you use the telegraph? It would be faster, or telephone the sheriff in Rapid City if you have one," Maka suggested.

"We don't have a phone yet."

Maka wrote down the Rapid City address.

"How old are you?" he asked.

"I'm fourteen," Maka answered.

"Twelve," Wishiwu said.

"Mighty pretty girls," he said. "You could make some money and friends here," he said.

"Now, now," Miss Alice interrupted, "Let's not get into that. Sheriff can you get started on finding their parents for them?"

"Fine. Fine. Girls, I'll be back tonight. See you again." He nodded and was on his way.

"What did he mean make money?" Maka asked.

"You'll see," Miss Alice said, winking across the room at Molly, who winked back.

That night, Maka and Wishiwu were given trays of whiskey and asked to circulate among the crowd of men and women, offering them drinks, and writing down the tab for each man. Miss Molly gave them dresses like the other prostitutes wore, with blouses low on their shoulders to accentuate their breasts, of which Wishiwu was flat chested, but Maka had formed, small breasts.

"Oh, come on. Look at us," Maka smirked. "They want us to go out there like them, like little whores."

"She said she would pay us something. We might need some money. "

They wore white stockings that came up to the top of their knees and thick petticoats underneath the skirts. In this uniform, they carried a tray of drinks and nuts, stopping to offer to the brothel's patrons and the women.

"I am trying not to laugh at this costume," Maka whispered as Wishiwu walked past her. Miss Alice introduced the girls to the women as the night began, at 9 pm when the first customer entered the room, who waited patiently outside the front door until it opened. After a half an hour, there were seven prostitutes but only five potential customers to serve.

"These are all whores. Amazing!" Maka whispered to her sister, watching the women throw themselves at the men that came into the house. A man would enter, and Miss Alice took his hat and guns, and put them into a closet. Unoccupied girls vied for new customers and ask them to sit down and drink. The women ranged in age from the fourteen-year old Britt to the forty seven year old Cherry, who told her customers she was thirty-one. They were heavily rouged, perfumed and powdered. Two of them held hands and giggled, making secret fun of the patrons. Another, who had taken the name Tigress, could barely keep her eyes open.

The men were limited to three drinks and Miss Alice was strict about that. She made the rule after learning the hard way about drunken cowboys. She would not let Indians come into the house at all. The whores were served water with a drop of whiskey, but the men were charged for the whore's drinks as well.

"Every man walked in wants a piece of that one," Miss Alice whispered to Molly, nodding towards Maka as she dutifully handed out drinks. "Britt's got competition."

"This is pretty easy work for a dollar," Wishiwu said when they sat alone in the kitchen. "These men are so stupid, but some of them are nice. I hope father doesn't ever go to places like this. One man said I reminded him of his niece and asked me if I would go to the room with him."

"Yeah. They all are asking me to go a room, too. Miss Alice warned me. We know what goes on. I can't tell a man he's my student and ask him to feel my boobs."

"That man sucked on Molly like her baby or something."

"He put his thing into her. Remember what mother told us. Wait until we get married so if there is a baby it will have a father. She said men will try to get inside of you, but you must fight them off. "

"Remember the time we heard Mother and Father?"

"Yes. They thought we were asleep."

"How do these women keep from having babies?"

"We have to get out of here. They just walked in!"

The droopy-eyed cowboy and his freckled friend entered the room, whacking a cloud of dust off their clothes, and as they surveyed the crowd, saw Maka and Wishiwu straight away.

"Out the back!" Maka urged and Wishiwu followed her, through the kitchen and into the alley.

"Where to?"

"Steal some horses?"

Parked in the alley was the same wagon that transported them to Pierre, the cowboys' wagon.

"Let's take it!"

They climbed into the wagon and as soon as Maka untied the horses, a pistol cocked and a menacing voice warned," Not so fast!" Maka and Wishiwu faced Joseph and Andy, aiming their guns.

"You want to go for a ride? We'll take you for a ride. All the way to California. I'm tired of this. Do a better job tying them this time, Joseph!"

Back they went into the covered wagon, wrists tied, gagged and on the way to Omaha.

From the back of the bouncing two-horse wagon, Maka and Wishiwu heard the two men talking.

"Now what will we do with them? "

"I'm gonna marry the older one when we get to San Francisco."

"Yeah, right. "

"I am. Did you see her? She's beautiful."

"What am I supposed to do with the little one? Marry her? She's a child."

"You can watch her grow up."

"How are we gonna get on the train without them being tied up?"

"They know we will have their parents killed. Or we'll kill them too if they try. "

"May as well take the ties off then. We can't go on a train with two young girls tied up and gagged."

The droopy eyed Joseph crawled back into the wagon and untied them and took the gags off." You girls are coming with us on the train. Don't even try to escape cause we will kill your mother and father if you try. "

"You are despicable, ugly men!" Maka said.

"I may be ugly, but I'm not that other word," Joseph said, "And you are going to start liking me if you want to survive."

After he returned to his seat, Maka whispered in her sister's ear. "First chance we get. I'm not marrying that man! "

CHAPTER 6

❧

Leo McEver had never been in love nor had anyone ever loved him, but he didn't care. If he wanted to, he could buy love. From childhood, he recognized he was not blessed with the prettiest of faces. His rusty hair wanted to sprout in eight directions at once, so that he started a custom of smoothing it down with lard. It once became so matted that his father had to shave it all off with sheep shears.

His Boston family had money, but many of his school classmates had even more, so that he could not intimidate them with his wealth. That only gave him the growing determination to have more than anyone else, perhaps on the planet, so he could flaunt it in people's faces. His teeth did not cooperate in growing straight and his lower row appeared as a patchwork quilt of cavity-strewn cutters and his front two teeth ventured further and further apart as he grew.

He was already homely enough when his older brother Wyatt punched him in the nose and shattered it, leaving him with an indentation in the center of his face that caused labored breathing the rest of his life.

Thrown out of two schools, he still was intelligent and learned how to make money from his father. Leo's father owned a bank in the center of the Boston financial district, near the Quincy Market, and instructed his three sons on the process of loans and investments. Leo parlayed that knowledge into his business beginnings as a neighborhood loan shark, lending a dollar today for two dollars tomorrow and hiring two toughies as collection agents. He needed the support of thugs and bullies, because he was physically very weak, with a scrawny chest, narrow shoulders and indecipherable biceps.

His two older brothers, Wyatt and Lawrence, asked him to accompany them on their quest for California gold in 1849. They scored big, mainly by cheating another man out of his strike, then defrauding three other miners out of their claims by loaning them funds with a heavy payback. Finally, neither older brother could bear working with Leo and they dissolved their partnership when Leo became embroiled in an attempted rape case they had to buy his way out of.

Leo's own mother could not find a way to love her child, he was such a n'er do well.. She once was so mad when he was sent him from school, she screamed at him,

"I should have stopped at two. No, your father insisted. One more. We gotta get it right. Well, we went further wrong. How is it I brought into the world three bastards out of my own womb? "

Now he was 75 years old and his past was littered with assaults on women, scores of men cheated out of riches and several attempts on his life. A psychologist may have determined all he needed was for his mother to love him, but he hated his own mother, too.

In Boston, he didn't have enough money to impress the girls in his neighborhood, so he ventured into the slums and scouted for attractive young girls, bringing with him several dollars for them and his bullies to protect him. On one occasion, parents of a thirteen-year-old girl from the Bowery found their way to the McEver's front door, claiming Leo had offered marriage to their daughter, five hundred dollars in exchange for sex. She had delivered on her part of the bargain and they demanded Leo marry their daughter, out of fear she may become pregnant. That family was paid off, no pregnancy ever came. In fact, Leo never impregnated a woman in his life. He didn't have to submit to any testing to know that he was sterile.

This practice continued in San Francisco. They didn't have to love them; they had to pretend to like him. The whores that told him he was good looking earned extra pay. Even after his first two marriages, he was a regular at two brothels.

So, when his assistant Jenkins, pulled out the balance sheets and showed him the grim story of where the finances had gone, that was when he resurrected the idea of that strike his neighbor had scored and hidden. He needed a new source of cash or his whole empire was in jeopardy.

The move to Rapid City suited him just fine. It was a town he could run. The day he moved in, he was the richest man and he quickly set about buying the saloon, hotel and bank, putting the judge under his payroll. Nobody knew him from anywhere. He bought as much land as he could, hired miners to dredge the earth and found his bookkeeper and personal assistant, Jenkins.

He made frequent trips to San Francisco, his respite from the boredom of Rapid City. And one trip, he returned with a twenty-year-old prostitute with the new title of Mrs. McEver. She was cleverer than the others he paid for. She bargained for the sky. If it meant leaving California for the wastelands of South Dakota, a heavy price had to be paid.

Jenkins was a man of thirty years of age who grew up in Rapid City, had a knack for bookkeeping, and worked at the bank before Leo discovered his assistant skimming profits. McEver's nefarious ways did not bother him. Every once in a while, he was offered McEver's wife for the night. He knew McEver was strange in his sexual appetite, then again, at 75; it was no wonder hat voyeurism was his main obsession. McEver watched other men do what he could no longer do himself.

Jenkins revealed the bad news to McEver, in the period from 1895 to 1905, his fortune had declined to a mere ten percent of what he started with in Rapid City.

"Uh, Mr. McEver. The mines haven't produced revenue in four years, Rapid City is shrinking. It is time to make some changes."

McEver fired all but his most experienced miners, for they actively scoured Pettigrew's land for the possible site. He sold the hotel, but kept the saloon. The railroad was due to pass through Rapid City in a few years and that would bring more business. He just had to find a way to sustain until that time.

One afternoon a stately carriage parked in front of Brave Eagle and Onashola's small house. At nine o'clock on a Saturday morning. Mr.

McEver instructed the driver to take his wife into town, drop her off, and return while he talked to Onashola.

He walked with the aid of a cane and wore a bowler hat purchased on a trip to New York City. He knocked on the door, and when Onashola answered, the carriage pulled away.

"Hello, Mrs. Heard. A word?"

Onashola surprised at the visitor, asked. "What do you want?"

"May I come in?"

"We don't have any house like yours. The only place to sit is at the dining table." Onashola canned fruit at an oak table, on one side and McEver on the other. She wore a white blouse and denim skirt, without petticoats. He was dressed in a suit, and Onashola wondered why.

"I take it by now your daughters have not turned up."

"No."

"And your husband should be nearing San Francisco?"

"He made Omaha yesterday."

"You are a mighty handsome woman," he stared lustfully at her, and moved his cane to within an inch of her feet. "You are living alone, with only an old woman next door and no protection. Can I offer you some of my men to watch over you?"

"I don't need watching over!"

He took his cane, lifted it under her skirt, long enough to see the tanned thighs before her hand came crashing down with such force the cane cracked in two.

"Leave, Mr. McEver. Get out of here!"

He picked up the broken cane and appraised the damage.

"I should hire you as a bodyguard."

She stood and brushed her skirt, feeling violated.

"Go now."

He got up from his chair. "If anything ever happens to the half-breed husband of yours, you would be welcome at my ranch. And, might I add, in my bed."

"I am sure your wife would like that."

"Oh, I would make her watch."

"You are disgusting. You will regret what you say."

"It is more likely you will be the one apologizing to me, Mrs. Heard, can I call you Onashola? You will even beg me. And as for your husband, I could buy and sell him any day."

"Take your broken cane and leave!"

McEver walked out the door, but his carriage had not returned, so he sat on the porch until it returned.

"Sorry you waited," his young wife Josephine said, with a hint of a smirk in her voice. "What did you want?"

"Some old, unfinished business."

Mrs. Pettigrew gave Brave Eagle enough money to travel in relative style, purchasing a Pullman sleeping car seat. He sold his horse to a stable near the train station. He felt so stiff and tired; he thought he would sleep for two days straight. He carried his satchel, containing close to four hundred dollars and the valuable key.

"If I get to the bank before these men, what is there?" he had asked Mrs. Pettigrew.

"More money and some papers. I think the map is among the papers."

"What will you do with this map?"

"I want you to set it on fire. What good is a map of a mine to me? If it is on McEver's property, I don't want him to benefit of knowing where it is."

Brave Eagle speculated they took the western route, in which case he would arrive in San Francisco before them. If he beat them to the bank, he planned to take the key Mrs. Pettigrew gave him, and withdraw the material from the safe deposit box, and wait for the arrival of the men who took his daughters. Hopefully, they were still with them. If they weren't, he would tear their fingernails out until they revealed what the whereabouts of Maka and Wishiwu.

The Omaha train station was larger than the small little outside waiting areas in smaller towns. This station had a large inside waiting area for passengers. He approached the ticket window, his satchel over his shoulder. He realized he needed a bath, but could wait until he got to California. He bought a round-trip ticket and sat in a waiting area. It was nine a.m. and the westbound train would not depart until two p.m. So, he waited to see if the kidnappers showed up. Still, they could opt not to take the train at all, in which case he would have to wait a week for them to show up.

He held the ticket in his left hand and the satchel in his right. The rest of his life depended upon the successful mission - the safety of his daughters. He cared less about this map, but it was valuable to these men. Other passengers began to seat in the benches around him, but not the men he sought.

Thirty minutes before boarding, three cowboys came into the station, men Brave Eagle had seen before in Rapid City, and undoubtedly the cowboys he evaded. They arrived at the ticket window, and one surveyed the waiting areas. The man nudged another cowboy and pointed at Brave Eagle. He would have company on the train. The cowboys were McEver ranch hand. One of the men was Deadeye, who had the reputation of a gunslinger, escaped from an Arizona prison. They called him Deadeye because he wore an eye patch that covered an empty socket. A Lakota in the wars gouged out his eye, and he hated Indians. He searched for Brave Eagle, who moved away from his bench.

The other two were brothers named Sam and Bob Jones. All the ranch hands were rude troublemakers, the kind that would get drunk at the saloon, come outside and shoot their guns into the air for no reason other than nobody stopped them. The Jones brothers were thin and rangy, nervous types. They grew up in Rapid City, and been kicked out of the school in the fourth grade.

Brave Eagle had a seat on car number four, so he boarded car number seven and walked through the cars. The men would find him, but not until he found them first. It was always better to be the hunter than the hunted.

He found his seat, and his sleeping booth. He could not safely sleep in the booth. He imagined a pistol pointed at his nose in the night, and there would go the satchel. This ride would not include sleeping. His as-signed seat number seven, by the window, and an attractive woman, dark haired and in her thirties, came into the seat next to him. She wore a fur-lined jacket she removed and placed it on her lap. Her face was heav-ily rouged, but she only had a hint of perfume.

"Going far?" she asked.

"San Francisco. That's where this train goes, I hope," the question threw him. He was on the right train, he hoped.

"That's where I live."

" I don't live there, just visiting."

"I live in Berkeley, where my husband, rest his soul, taught."

"What did he teach?"

"He taught archeology. That is his life. Looking for dinosaurs. We spent the summers looking for bones. At least, he did. You have family in California?"

"No. I'm on business."

"My name is Mabel Morgan. What's yours?"

"Thomas Heard."

"Where are you from?"

"South Dakota," Brave Eagle answered, avoiding her penetrating gaze.

"Where Custer was killed."

"Yes," Brave Eagle answered with a slight smile.

"Had to be terrible. Surrounded by thousands of Indians. That's why I rarely go west of Omaha. I'm afraid of getting scalped. Is it safe now?"

"Depends on what you mean by safe. Is Omaha safe?"

"Parts of the city I won't go to."

"Why not? Would you get scalped?"

"Most likely robbed."

Brave Eagle grew quiet for a while, and she asked. "Are you married?"

"Yes, I am. And two daughters."

"That's nice. We had no children. Still, I'm only twenty-nine, so if I re-marry. I'm not too old."

They continued talking until Mabel Morgan fell asleep. The train had been gone an hour, and Brave Eagle needed to explore. In his car, were eight sleeping bins and eight seats. With these men on board, there would be no sleep.

He walked back through the train, still carrying his satchel, passing through the Pullman sleeping cars to the second-class cabins. He entered each car. Six cars back, he took a step into a car, and the three cowboys sat in two seats facing each other, but sleeping. Brave Eagle was so fatigued himself; he barely kept his eyes open. So, he returned to the Pullman car. He chose to sleep in number eight because there were no passengers assigned that booth. He tucked his satchel in the corner of the booth for a pillow, and fell asleep, his knife and loaded pistol within reach.

All six of the passengers slept in their compartments, and Brave Eagle rested, but did not sleep. Then, he heard them.

"The conductor said seat five and the booth is back here."

"Behind the curtains. They're all asleep."

Brave Eagle was in the top right bunk and as they peered into the bottom left bunk, he jumped out of the booth, and ran out of the car.

"Hey!"

He ran into the vestibule between the two cars, and climbed the ladder to the top of the car, and he lay down atop the car, his face battered by a hard and windy rain.

From the top of the car, he saw the two men go through the vestibule into the next car towards the engine. Brave Eagle walked his arms extended for balance, from the top of the train towards the caboose. The wind howled and the rain beat his face in sheets. As the rain scorched his face, a gust of wind almost took him off the train, but he held fast to a handhold built into the top of the car.

That was close. He had to find his daughters, and once he found them, he would never let them out of his sight again. Hurl the rain down on me, God, he thought. Test me. If I am to be another Job, you can test my strength, for I will not give in.

He crossed each car, climbed down the ladder and up the ladder to the next car. The train crossed a bridge over a vast river, and he lay down on top of the train. He passed over five cars, before descending into a car behind the men and entered the car. As he climbed down the ladder to the vestibule, a hand grabbed his calf.

"I got you!"

It was Deadeye, and he stepped back as Brave Eagle put his steps on the platform, and held a pistol at Brave Eagle's nose, but Brave Eagle struck his fist upward, knocking the pistol into the air, and grabbed the man by the collar.

The man clutched at Brave Eagle's satchel and tried to wrench it from across Brave Eagle's shoulder, and as he did, Brave Eagle pushed him. Deadeye started to fall off the train, grabbed Brave Eagle's shirt and pulled him and they fell off the train together.

They hit the ground with a thud and a loud clanking sound, of the man's skull hitting the rail of the second track. Brave Eagle bounced off the man into a gulley on the other side of the tracks. The rain battered, and as the train sped away, he walked over to the still man on the other tracks and put his fingers to the man's neck. Brave Eagle noticed a cavalry pin on the man's collar. Maybe they had a horse for him to ride in Heaven. Brave Eagle dragged him off the track, took the man's holster and gun, searched his pockets and only found ten dollars and a sheet of paper with the address of the First San Francisco Bank.

Maka and Wishiwu watched the countryside roll by, mile by mile. The train passed through the splendor of the Rocky Mountains in Colorado, momentarily diverting their attention from their plans to escape. They were constantly under observation and every visit from a conductor heightened their anxiety. They found towels in their sleeping quarters that served as shawls to cover their chests, but still wore the brothels' petticoats.

Andy and Joseph alternated sleep duty – when Maka and Wishiwu slept in the top bank, they took turns with one asleep in the bottom bunk and the other awake on the outside of the bunk.

Maka once lowered her head to check if they were awake.

"Don't think about it," Joseph warned.

Maka whispered to her sister, "When we get off the train. They can't run with us. If only one of us escapes, get to a sheriff. They'll be headed to the bank. What was it?"

"First."

"Right. So, the issue will be to get back to South Dakota. To get a ticket when the men might be taking the same train back. That's what they have to do, too, get back to South Dakota."

"Think about it. They intended to go to the bank and bring us back. If we go back first, then what? There's going to be a battle back home. What a dumb plan!"

"Yeah. These men are not exactly the smartest. They are leading their way to their own Little Big Horn."

Lying in the bunk was their only chance to talk.

"I hate to think what will happen to these men when brave Eagle catches them."

"Oh, he's probably already in San Francisco. He had time to get ahead of us."

"This is insane, the whole thing. Wouldn't it be funny if this box in the bank had nothing inside? Here we are, hostages, over a piece of paper."

Andy and Joseph managed to keep Maka and Wishiwu under control during the ride from Omaha to San Francisco by alternating sleep shifts and operating under the threat that if they tried to escape, it would be Brave Eagle and Onashola who paid.

But Maka convinced Wishiwu they should try to escape. The opportunity came as they descended the step off their train car in the San Francisco Union station. Joseph, holding Maka with one hand, carried a satchel in the other and as he stepped off the train, his satchel became tangled with another passenger behind him, and he lost his grip and it dropped. He let go of Maka, but the other passenger, in trying to help Joseph, got in the way and in one swift move, Maka grabbed the satchel, "Now!" She shoved Andy who turned and Wishiwu twisted free of his grip. They ran and Joseph yelled, "Stop those thieves!"

The girls' speed and endurance far exceeded the two men burdened by their duffle bags. The girl emerged from the station, encountered a line of horse-drawn carriages and climbed into the first one.

"Where do you want to go?" the driver asked.

Maka shrugged, "The Ocean!"

"The wharf?"

"Yes."

"What's in the satchel?" Wishiwu leaned in.

Maka opened the satchel and saw a wad of money. "Joseph's share. They will kill each other over the rest."

"Now what?" Wishiwu asked.

"We have to find a way home. They are going to the bank they talked about tomorrow. Maybe we better stay here a couple of days or we risk running into them at the train station."

"Won't the sheriff put them in jail?"

" Sounded like they will never return."

As the carriage idled towards the ocean, Maka peered at the throngs of people. "We could get lost in here."

The carriage took them down Market Street to the piers. The streets had all kinds of transportation: horse-drawn carriages, automobiles and cable cars. Maka and Wishiwu marveled at all the sights, sounds and smells of the city.

"Amazing, isn't it?"

"Where will we stay? We don't know anyone here."

"A hotel. We have money," Maka shrugged.

"But how do you get into a hotel?"

"Money. Same as anything else. They won't ask questions if we have money. Let's get some clothes first. Do you know of a clothing store?" Maka leaned out of the carriage to ask the driver.

The driver dropped them at a store on Market Street, and Maka and Wishiwu traded in their petticoats for more demure outfits.

"We look like the Little Women of Louisa May Alcott," Maka laughed, modeling her white ruffled blouse buttoned under her chin and her broad denim skirt.

"That's better than looking like Moll Flanders!"

The satchel tight under Maka's arm, they walked past scores of homeless beggars, tin cans extended.

"Never seen this before," Wishiwu observed, "Should we give them some?"

"There's too many. Besides, this is Miss Pettigrew's money, really."

"Well, her husband got it from the Black Hills, and whose land is that?"

"Good point. But look at them all. "

"That might be us if you didn't grab that bag. "

They stepped over an entire family of three young children in rags, when a toothless hag confronted them. She smelled of the rotted fish she had just eaten from a trash bin.

"What that bag got?"

As the old woman stopped them, with one swift motion, a blade ripped the satchel strap and a teenaged boy took off with it.

"Get him?"

The old woman stuck out her leg and tripped Maka as the boy ran, and tried to grab Wishiwu, but the two girls sped off in pursuit. The boy crossed the street and had a good fifty yards on Maka, who quickly closed the gap. He turned down into an alley and ran into a dead end, when Maka reached him, followed by Wishiwu.

"You want this? Come and get it!" He showed his knife.

Maka looked at the boy, all skin and bones, wearing dirty rags that substituted for clothes. He had no shoes and his feet bled from the run. The boy looked at a wall behind him. "You girls ain't gonna stop me!"

"Drop it now!" Maka saw a rock on the ground, picked it up and prepared to throw.

"Drop it or I'll throw!"

"What's in here you want so bad?" he looked inside the satchel and as he did, Maka hurled a strike that clanked the boy right between the eyes. The boy collapsed, out cold.

"Wow! Good throw!" Maka and Wishiwu leaned over the boy and turned him over.

"Is he dead?"

Maka placed her fingertips on the boy's wrist. "Nope. That's gonna hurt, but he asked for it." She pulled the satchel from his grasp.

"I'm hiding this under my blouse somehow. All these poor people here. They must all come to California for the weather. I never saw people like this in South Dakota."

"Too cold there to beg."

"We better be careful. This city is different from what we're used to."

"There's evilness everywhere. Andy and Joseph ought to stay here and live. They'd fit right in!"

They walked from the back alley back to market Street, crossing to the other side to avoid more beggars and finally reached the pier, where they sat on the dock.

"Look! Seals!" Wishiwu pointed to a rock near the pier where a half dozen seals languished in the sun.

"They look like big fat black slugs."

A seal barked in protest.

"Ha! I never thought we'd ever see a seal. Let's get our feet in the water!"

They continued down the wharf until they found a way to get into the water. The sun was setting, but there were a handful of swimmers on a short stretch of beach. Maka and Wishiwu walked ankle deep.

"The Pacific Ocean! And what it took to get here. Let's promise we'll come back some day."

"Promise," Wishiwu twisted her little finger around Maka's.

They sat on the sand and watched the sunset, holding hands. "We better find a hotel. We're not sleeping here where these homeless people can get us. Then, tomorrow, we wire home and tell them we got loose from those men."

CHAPTER 7

——— ⚜ ———

THE STREETS WERE filled with motorcars, something only the very rich had in South Dakota, and the cars wove around horse carriages and trolley cars. Maka handled the hotel registration process, approaching the desk clerk with cash in the palm of her hand.

"I would like a room for three days, please," she told the man at the front desk, a young man of about twenty, dressed in a red vest and bow tie.

He motioned to the big open book on the counter. "Sign the register, Miss. We have a room with one bed on the fourth floor, facing the street."

"Fine."

"That will be nine dollars in advance for three nights. Here is the key. If you ever leave the hotel, be sure and drop the key at the front desk."

They carried no luggage, but a bellman took them to their room by boarding the first elevator the sisters ever rode. They kept their excitement constrained until alone in the room and they laid back atop the bed together.

"What a city! There are only four automobiles in Rapid City; must be four thousand here! " Wishiwu exclaimed.

Brave Eagle believed the best option was to follow the tracks until he got to the next town, where he could re-board and continue west. Which meant a twenty-four hour delay in his plans. On the other side of the gulley was a wooded area, and he found a clump of trees offered cover from the storm. He took off his soaked clothes, and changed into a dry shirt and some linen pants. He had a canteen in his satchel and left it to collect rainwater while he slept.

He awoke at daybreak. The rain stopped and the humidity sweltered at six in the morning. He wondered if and when Deadeye would be discovered. There was no sign of any civilization. He had no family that would miss him, as McEver always hired derelicts and misfits.

He ran on the tracks. Running was not easy carrying the satchel; so after about thirty minutes, he walked. He could walk forty miles in a day. The heat bore down on him, and the canteen proved to be a lifesaver as the day arched close to 100 degrees.

After several hours, He reached a river bridge and saw a town across the river. The river bridge was tricky to cross and to slip meant one long swim. Paddleboats chugged into the dock across the river and a large barge carrying coal drifted by. The town was Burlington, Iowa, and when he arrived at the train station at one p.m., he found he would wait six hours for the next train, so he ventured into the town and found a dry goods store where he purchased a pair of jeans and another shirt. He ate a meal of potatoes and gravy and a steak, and felt refreshed.

There was a Western Union office in the train station and he sent a telegraph to Onashola in Rapid City. "On the train to San Francisco. No sign of them on the way here."

He bought another ticket, again getting a sleeping booth, and when he boarded the train, climbed into the relative comfort of his sleeping quarters.

Union station in San Francisco was thousands of people who all seemed to know where they were going. It was a sea current of people and he climbed the stairs to the street. He asked a couple who stared out at the city, tourists, if they knew the way to Market Street, and they didn't. They said they came from Des Moines. Then, he asked a man in a business suit who gave directions.

San Francisco was mammoth. Some of the tribe elders had been to Washington to meet with the White Chief and had an understanding of the enormity of trying to fight back this swelling tide of people. He came upon a big store and made up his mind to dress as a businessman, and in disguise, pass by the McEver ranch hands.

He emerged looking the part of a banker. A black suit, white shirt, shined shoes, and a fedora hat. Still, he carried his satchel, which carried 2 guns, his knife and old clothes. He found a barber, where he got his hair trimmed and his face shaved. It was afternoon by the time he made it to the bank and saw on the Market Street side, Sam Jones, one of McEver's men. He waited for a stream of people, put the fedora down over his eyes, and walked briskly into the bank.

He was shown the way to the safe deposit room to sign a log and display the key. A man retrieved the box and left him alone in the room. There were two envelopes in the box; one full of money, tens of thousands of dollars. The other contained a sheath of papers, and Brave Eagle perused the papers and found a map of the Black Hills.

Mrs. Pettigrew instructed him to open a bank account, so he drafted a check once he got to South Dakota, rather than carrying money back across the country, so he exited the safe deposit area and sat down with a banker to open an account. He sat in a room with the banker who was impressed with the size of the deposit, as he counted out seventy five thousand and forty dollars. Through the window of the office, Brave Eagle saw the McEver man, glaring at him.

Brave Eagle kept one thousand dollars and the papers, which he figured were what the man was after. So, the money deposited, the next quest was how to get past the two men. Mrs. Pettigrew told him to stay at the Victoria, a prestigious hotel near the piers.

He signed the bank deposit form and right at the moment he stood away from the desk, a shot rang out in the street. The McEver man rushed for the door.

"Is there another way out of the bank?" Brave Eagle asked the teller.

"Come with me." He led Brave Eagle to a side door, and opened it to the street. Brave Eagle withdrew a knife from the satchel and into the palm of his hand and walked around the corner, where the McEver man stood over the fallen body of another ranch hand. Brave Eagle crossed the street.

A voice said "Hey! Brave Eagle! I'll take that!"

Andy and Joseph, the two thugs from Rapid City, stood in front of him, and a pistol square in his stomach.

Joseph stood behind Brave Eagle, a gun at his back. The street was crowded with people, on their way to work or shopping.

"So you had a key, too? Pretty good work, huh, Joseph? We're not off the train more than an hour and now we got what's in the bag. That map McEver wants so bad he sends two more men after us. "

Brave Eagle handed the satchel to Andy. "Where are my daughters?"

"Wouldn't you like to know?" Andy reached inside the satchel. "Here's a wad of bills, and an envelope, which I am sure we can use."

"We got what we came for, Andy? What do we do with him?"

"I think the police are all occupied with our friend over there. What's another shooting?"

"Too many people, Andy."

"I only want my daughters. You can have the bag."

"Start walking."

The pier loomed ahead. "I hope you are a good swimmer," Andy said.

As they took a few steps into the pier, Brave Eagle spun towards Joseph, slapping the pistol from his grasp into the water. Andy turned and Brave Eagle threw his knife straight into his heart. Joseph took a step to flee, but Brave Eagle grabbed him by the neck, and picked him up by his shirt collar, holding him over the edge of the pier.

"Where are my daughters?

"They got away!" Joseph stared at the dirty brown river, thirty feet below.

"Where?"

"Here At the station, they ran. Let me up, please. I'm just a hired hand."

"Who are these other men?"

"He sent them, to get us."

A policeman ran in his direction, so he dropped Joseph on the pier, grabbed the satchel and ran. Later, he found a Western Union office where he wired Onashola, "Maka and Wishiwu escaped the men. They are here somewhere." He walked back to the train station, and tried to visualize where his daughters might go. At the Western Union office, he wired Rapid City to Onashola. "In San Francisco. Girls escaped men and I look for them. Got the box at the bank." After scouring the train station to make sure they were not there, he walked the four miles back to the hotel.

Once, at the South Dakota state fair, there was a 50-dollar prize if anyone took down a 350-pound giant wrestler, and man after man put up the two-dollar entrance fee. The wrestler swatted them away, some of them with broken bones. Brave Eagle said to Onashola and his daughters who were about ten and eight at the time, "I can take him down."

Onashola smiled, "Fifty dollars. Don't get hurt!"

Brave Eagle entered the ring and stayed about six feet distance, circling the hulk of a man, who had a shaven head and arms as big as Brave Eagle's thighs. Brave Eagle feinted to the left and the wrestler went for the move, but Brave Eagle followed the wrestlers momentum, leapt into the air and with his legs scissor-kicked the man's legs and he toppled to the ground. Brave Eagle hopped on the man's back, twisted his massive arm behind his back, buried his own head into the nape of the man's neck and pulled back on his head.

"OWW! I give; you're going to break my neck! Stop!" the man shrieked.

A referee lifted Brave Eagle's arm in victory.

"Less than sixty seconds. You are only the second man to beat him in five years," the referee shouted.

Brave Eagle shrugged. Crazy Horse could have done the same thing, since it was his move Brave Eagle used.

When confronted with danger, there was always a way out, to escape. He coached his daughters, trained them on fighting and the use of every weapon. Why? Because solitude and peace are never something to take for granted. He had been on the winning side at Little Big Horn, but if not for circumstances; he might have been on the losing side. If his father had decided to take him away from the reservation, he might have been raised white and become a soldier. What if he had been a soldier at Little Big Horn?

He settled that first night in San Francisco into his luxurious bed, plotting the next day's search for his daughters. The mangle of humanity he encountered on his way to the hotel only convinced him that this way of life was not for him. His was the Lakota way and that was of quiet wisdom, in harmony with the earth and this place, despite its beautiful setting, appeared to be boiling.

The white world's desire for wealth and riches was a foreign concept – to have more and more land, money, things. For someone who spent most of his life living in a fifty square foot tipi, the extravagant homes were a waste of space.

Perhaps he should have spent more time growing up in his father's world if he were to understand it all, but his father also claimed he was more comfortable with the Lakota than his own people. Brave Eagle was a master of humility and simplicity. It was not his way to brag over his accomplishments. The Lakota had a night they called waktoglaka, when each of them stood before the campfire and recounted their adventures and successes. Brave Eagle always sat on the side, knowing that only one other brave could match his battle successes. Crazy Horse was another who never participated, because everyone knew because he led every charge. Only two braves knew the true killer of Custer and the legend grew that it was Crazy Horse, and this was one time he did not bother to correct those stories, for in many ways, he killed Custer by outwitting him, or even more to the point, Custer outwitted himself.

There was no way the size of a city; the size of the entire earth would prevent him from tracking his daughters and reuniting the family. He was past sixty years old, and happiness had never visited him until he and Onashola discovered each other. There was some purpose in their survival and there was some purpose in this very mission, what he was yet to discover.

If it was God he could credit for giving him the gift of Onashola, Maka and Wishiwu, then he worshiped at that altar. That concept the Lakota called the Great Mystery. In Onashola, he had the perfect mate. She reminded him of the legend of No Moccasins. Her husband, the warrior Three Horns, was believed killed on the raid of another tribe. No Moccasins did not believe her husband could die and leave her alone on this earth, so she set out alone and in the night, discovered where three Horns was held prisoner. She cut his ties and they escaped and to send the chasing braves off their trail, left her moccasins by a creek, continuing the journey home without shoes, thus attaining her name and legend.

He and Onashola had discussed the wisdom of leaving her in Rapid City while he went to San Francisco. She remained home in case Maka and Wishiwu returned on their own. They cold not imagine that any of the dimwitted cowboys could hold their daughters prisoner for very long. They had picked the wrong family to mess with.

Despite his aging body, Brave Eagle felt fully in charge of his powers and senses in this quest. Before this, his life had become the picture of tranquility, peace and books. Now, there was a heightened awareness. The hunter had returned.

Brave Eagle remembered fondly when Betty Pettigrew gave his daughters porcelain dolls for Christmas, with eyelids that opened and closed. The girls played for hours with their two dolls, naming them Annie and Hester. Watching them grow filled him with a joy he had never experienced in all his days and now Maka surpassed Onashola in height, while Wishiwu still had growing to do.

He carried some spectacles for reading and in next to the hotel bed, there was the Bible. So, he would read the Bible until he slept. It seemed a crime that he slept in such a soft bed, worrying that his daughters were loose on the streets, when in reality they also slept in a different hotel, a mere four blocks distant. Brave Eagle had never stayed a night in a hotel, much less slept on a mattress the size of the hotel's, which could have accommodated four people quite easily. He slept in some long underwear he had purchased with his business suit and placed the satchel and his clothes next to the bed.

But the luxury was short-lived. In the night, there was a violent rumble and shake

And the bed flipped upside down on top of Brave Eagle and when the dust cleared, he lay beneath the mattress, covered in dust and soot.

Earlier that day, McEver, one of the first in Rapid City to own a phone, received a phone call from his lone man in San Francisco.

"He got away, Mr. McEver."

"And how did that happen?"

"We waited at the bank and Joseph and Andy showed up at the same time Brave Eagle was in the bank. Andy shot Dave and Brave Eagle got away in the confusion."

"Why didn't you check the Hotel?"

"I got tied up with Dave."

"Where is Joseph?"

"Probably here somewhere. There's plenty of whorehouses. I bet he can be found there."

"Never mind about him. Just come back."

"Sorry, boss. We tried. Who knew we would get ambushed?"

McEver hung up the phone and turned to his top aide. "They botched the job. If he comes back here with those papers, our lovely Mrs. Pettigrew could own this ranch. Dear Mrs. Pettigrew. I am afraid Brave Eagle just sealed her death warrant."

The Sheriff knocked on Onashola's door and she opened it. Bone knew the sheriff and sniffed the scent of the sheriff's dog on his leg.

"Down, Bone. Hello, Sheriff. What is it?"

"Mind if I come in? I have good news and bad news."

Onashola's breath grew heavy. "It's them. Where are they?" she asked as she escorted him to a chair at the kitchen table.

"Well, they were in Pierre. But they are gone now."

"Pierre? Not far!"

"They were last seen at a whore house. But they ran away from some men there and have not been seen."

Onashola grasped the kitchen table for support and sat.

"What?"

'Now I don't know why they were there or what. But we won't know until they turn up and they went on the run and nobody knows where they are."

The next day, the letter arrived from Maka, telling Onashola they were in San Francisco and Onashola went directly to the Wire office to leave a wire for Brave Eagle.

She sat down with Betty Pettigrew on the front porch with Bone, rocking on two chairs. It was unusually warm for an April evening, about 55 degrees.

"I finally get a phone in tomorrow. That will help."

"How does it work when somebody calls you from another state?"

"They ask the operator to reverse the charges."

"Wherever my daughters are, when Brave Eagle finds them...I just have to talk to them. What could have possibly happened? "

"Those girls could take care of themselves. You're looking awfully frail, Onashola. Remember to eat."

"Oh, who can eat at a time like this? Forget food! I want my daughters back!" She wept, and Miss Pettigrew patted her head.

That night, as Mrs. Pettigrew slept, two men crept up to her house. They threw a rock into the front window and tossed a torch inside. Then they went around to the back of the house, broke another window and threw another torch.

Bone, next door, barked incessantly and Onashola woke. She went out to the front of her house and saw the flames inside Mrs. Pettigrew's house. As she took a step off her porch and the men grabbed her, placed a chloroform-laced handkerchief over her mouth and she passed out.

Mrs. Pettigrew heard the dog and smelled the smoke. She got out of bed in her nightgown and went into the living room that was ablaze and impassable. She went to the back of the house and smoke grew thick. She covered her mouth with her arm, and opened a window and crawled out. A wagon hurried away down the road to the north, as she watched her house burn. It was four hundred yards to the nearest house, and she ran there, knocking on the door, awaking her neighbors, but by the time the volunteer fireman arrived the house was destroyed.

CHAPTER 8

---　❧　---

"I WANT TO go home," Wishiwu sighed, laying back on the bed next to her sister, pulling up the covers.

They slept, anxious about the future. At a little after 5 in the morning, a rumbling sound vibrated and the bed began to shake. They sat up and the bed moved violently, like a bucking bronco and threw them both to the floor. The room shook and plaster from the ceiling fell down upon them.

The room shifted sideways and the nightstand toppled over.

"Let's get out of here!" Maka screamed.

They crawled to the door, but the door was jammed shut.

"What's happening?" Wishiwu yelled. It sounded like a freight train storming through their room.

"An earthquake!"

The tremor lasted forty or forty five seconds. The room was full of dust so thick they could hardly breathe.

"We're not on the top floor any more. We're almost on the ground."

They heard screams and moans in the building.

"People are hurt!"

They took the sheets from the bed and tied them to make a rope long enough to reach the ground, only about fifteen feet down. They threw the blanket from the bed to the ground.

"Get the money from the mattress!"

Maka stashed the money into a satchel and they descended the makeshift rope. After they both made it down, a wall of bricks tumbled over and they scurried out of harm's way.

Dust coated the street and people walked to veer away from the falling buildings. The streets were eerily silent, as everyone prepared for another shock.

The street rose and fell, in rolling waves like the sea. As the ground swelled beneath them, they were thrown to the ground. The second tremor lasted only about ten seconds,

"Let's get away from the buildings, to the bay," Maka said.

Dawn broke and as they walked silently, hundreds of people surrounded them, walking like lemmings to the sea. A horse-drawn fire truck, clanging its bells towards the ferry building, passed them.

They walked only a couple of blocks, when Wishiwu tugged at Maka's arm.

"Listen."

A young boy cried nearby, coming from an alley.

"Momma...momma..."

A little boy sat shivering in short pants, next to a pile of fallen bricks. In the dim light, Maka and Wishiwu made out an outstretched hand, and a splayed leg, pinned by the bricks. No sounds came from the two bodies.

He was a towheaded boy, a shock of blonde hair, wearing an unbuttoned blue cardigan sweater.

"Help my momma and poppa. Please!"

Wishiwu held the boy to her. "We'll try to get the bricks off them."

The three of them began pulling bricks off. Maka started tossing them aside. She pulled a few bricks off the woman and gasped.

"Take him away, Wishiwu."

The woman's head was flattened by the bricks and crushed beyond recognition. Maka put bricks back over the woman's face so the boy could not see. Maka uncovered a red purse protruded from the pile. The man's shoes were visible.

"Little boy," Maka turned to Wishiwu who held the sobbing boy. " Your momma and poppa went to Heaven."

"Please, no!"

"They are gone," Maka said gently. "What is your name?'

"Bobby."

"Bobby what?"

"Bobby Lambert."

"Where do you live?"

"1855 Elmwood Street."

"In San Francisco?"

"No. Denver."

"What are you doing here?"

"We came to hear Caruso."

"Who?"

"A singer in the Opera."

Did anyone else come with you? Brothers and sisters?"

"No."

"Do you have any other family in Colorado?"

"An aunt."

"Where does the aunt live?"

"Denver."

"You better come with us now," Wishiwu held the boy's hand. He let go of Wishiwu and ran back. He pulled at his father's shoes, and Maka and Wishiwu pulled him away.

"Oh no, no, no."

He continued to weep, and did not want to leave his parents, but they led him away, as the masses walked in the street, away from buildings. The crowd was eerily quiet, many carrying whatever possessions they gathered in a minute's time. One woman carried a sewing machine. A little boy carried a cardboard box containing five newborn puppies, and his father carried the dog's mother, a man held a rocking chair over his head, perhaps his favorite possession. By the time Maka, Wishiwu and Bobby walked to the blazing ferry building.

They walked for hours, following people who paraded towards Fort Mason, as a sanctuary. They climbed a big hill that led into the fort, and from the perch at the top of the hill, saw smoke rising in several locations.

They settled on a patch of grass where a number of people rested and watched the city burn.

Maka sat upon the ground with her sister, and pulled the blanket over them for warmth.

"What are we going to do now?" Wishiwu asked. "They will never find us."

"It appears that has been decided. We're going to Denver on the way to South Dakota."

"Then, what do we do?"

"We find Bobby's aunt. We'll find a way to send a letter to momma and poppa telling them where we are going and give them an address. How old are you, Bobby?"

"Almost six."

"Bobby, we'll take you to Colorado. Did you live in a house?"

'Yes."

The boy's face was streaked with dust and traces of tears, and Maka and Wishiwu were also covered in dust and plaster. Maka took Wishiwu long black hair and swatted some of the dust away.

"Do I look as dirty as you?"

"Oh, yes."

"We need knives. We'll be sleeping out in the open."

As families congregated on the lawn, they spread out as if preparing for a picnic, blankets on the ground, looking back at the burning city. Maka and Wishiwu picked a spot near a family of a man, his wife, and two teen-aged sons.

"Are you alone?" the woman of the family asked.

"We are three of us," Maka answered. "Can we stay by you?'

"Of course. Where are your parents?"

"South Dakota."

"You here by yourselves?"

"Not our choice."

"How will they find you?"

"We're going to take our cousin.... I don't know," Maka could not make up a story.

"I think you should find your way to the train station. Everything is chaotic here. This is like the end of the world. One more shake and this whole city will fall into the sea."

"That's what we will do. Tomorrow. But we are too tired now to go anywhere."

"This place is safe enough. They are giving out canvas tents."

"Do you have a knife?"

"Tom?"

He nodded and reached into a bag of tools, handing Maka a nine-inch blade.

They stayed two days. So many fires swept the city that a trek to the train station was out of the question. A community of refugees from the earthquake emerged in the park lawn. There was no running water, no electricity, nothing but what the people carried on their backs and with their hands.

On the second day, a number of people watched a few men play baseball down the hill. There was a baseball diamond, a fence and some bleachers.

"You should show them your pitching," Wishiwu suggested to Maka.

"Guard the bags."

Maka walked up to a man watching from behind the backstop, who appeared to be the manager, since he kept barking instructions to the players.

"Can I play, too?"

"Sorry, kid. We're the San Francisco Seals ball club. Our field got destroyed, so we're practicing here until we find somewhere else to play. Besides, you're a girl."

"None of you can hit me!"

"Did you hear? Hey, Rico, this girl says no one can hit her!"

Rico, the first baseman smiled and nodded.

"Go sit down kid."

"But I can throw much faster."

"This is batting practice."

"Let me show you."

The manager shrugged. "Okay, Bart this girl insists she can throw batting practice. What do we have to lose? Let's go, kid." He led Maka to the pitcher's mound and the pitcher handed her the baseball.

"Can I have a mitt?"

"Here, David. Give her your glove. Take a rest."

"How hard do you want me to throw?"

"Throw as hard as you can. Do you think you can reach the catcher?"

"Of course."

"Take a few warm-ups."

The manager yelled at the batter. "Donnie, step back and let her throw one to the catcher."

The batter stepped away from the plate and Maka tossed softly to the catcher, but the ball bounced in the dirt.

"Sorry," Maka commented. "I haven't thrown a ball since last summer."

The catcher threw it back to her. She wound and threw a little harder and smacked the center of the catcher's mitt.

"A strike," the manager nodded.

Maka threw two more pitches in the same location, and turned to the manager. "I can throw with the batter now."

"Okay. Donnie take a swing."

Wishiwu shouted from the seats, "Throw a hard one, Maka!"

Maka leaned in, went into the windup and hurled a bullet to the catcher. The ball cracked loudly into the catcher's mitt. Donnie, the batter, reacted way too late and swung feebly at the pitch. "Jesus Christ! Did you see that?"

The catcher laughed. "Hey, Alfred. She's almost as fast as anyone in the PCL!"

"Do it again," the manager said.

Maka shrugged, wound up, and the same result. "Shit!" the batter winced.

"Strike two!" Wishiwu hollered.

"Again!" Alfred, the manager commanded.

Maka threw with all her might and the ball started low, and started rising, as the batter swung under and missed. "Did you see the movement?"

"Strike three!" Wishiwu cheered.

"Hey, Rico. You hit," Alfred coaxed.

Rico traded places with the batter Donnie, who moved over to first base.

Rico was a burly man. Six feet three and two hundred forty pounds.

Maka flung the ball around eighty miles an hour and Rico swung and tipped the ball foul, behind the catcher.

"Somebody finally got some wood on the ball," the catcher chuckled. "She could play for us now!"

"Maybe cut her hair and say she's a man," Rico offered, as he missed the second pitch.

"Two strikes on the big man!" Wishiwu yelled.

"Can you throw a curve?" Alfred asked.

"I can. I twist my wrists when I let go."

'Let's see."

Maka turned her wrist as she released. The ball came at Rico and he stepped back, but the ball curved right into the catcher's mitt. "STEE-RIKE!" the catcher laughed. "Shit. She's the best pitcher in the PCL if we sign her."

"Hey, Bart, you take over pitching batting practice. I want to talk to. What's your name?"

"Maka."

The manager put his hand on her shoulder and walked over to the bleachers with her and they sat down.

"I don't know if there is a rule against women in our league. You can make a lot of money playing ball."

Maka nodded. "I can make a lot of money doing a lot of things. But playing baseball?"

"You would join our team. We play all around the west in the Pacific Coast league. That batter you struck out is leading the league in hitting. Three eighty. "

"I'm sorry Mister. I don't think so. "

"By the way, how old are you?"

"Eighteen," she lied.

"Where are your parents?'

"South Dakota. We got taken from our home and made our way here. This earthquake happened and we found this little boy, Bobby. So now we want to take him to Colorado where his aunt lives and get our parents to meet us."

"The Seals are going to move to Oakland until we rebuild the stadium in San Francisco, but let me give you my name and address, Maka. And when you re ready to play ball, you contact me. We may cut off all your hair and say you are named Mickey."

"Mister. We can use some help getting to the train station."

"Oh, I'm going after practice to meet some of our players. Wait around, I'll take you."

So, Maka, Wishiwu and their new little friend, Bobby, were escorted in motorcars arranged to take the San Francisco Seals to Oakland. They quenched their thirst with a gallon of grape juice, their first drinks in two days.

They were dropped at the train station, where they bought three tickets to Denver. The station was mobbed with fleeing Californians, eager to escape San Francisco. The fatalities numbered three or four thousand. More than half the city was homeless. There was no water, no gas, and no electricity.

They waited in a long line to send a wire, which they got off to Rapid City.

Brave Eagle found himself pinned beneath his mattress from the chest down, dust and plaster thick over his head. He stretched to reach his satchel and pull it to him but could not quite grasp it. He pushed himself up and as he lifted the mattress, a second, even more violent quake struck and the whole building shook and caved.

He heard moaning and screaming nearby and for a moment, all was black. The mattress was still on top of him, but so was added weight. His head ached from hitting the floor with force and he felt like his brain was almost loose inside his head. After coming to his senses, he managed to squirm his body out from under the rubble.

He sifted through the splintered wood and plaster and located his satchel and the trousers from his business suit, then his shoes, and mustered the strength to emerge from the wrecked hotel. A woman lay dead on the street and a man hovered over her. Brave Eagle realized the man was trying to pull her wedding ring from her finger and shouted.

"Get away!"

"What's it to you? She's dead!" The man's face was smeared with sweat and dirt and his clothes were ripped to shreds.

"Go!"

"I'm not!"

Brave Eagle grabbed the man at the waist, lifted him and threw him down.

"Leave the dead woman!"

The man fled.

What Brave Eagle saw when he reached Market Street was an avenue of half naked, panicked people, and horses running scared. A long horned steer came barreling down the street, right at him and he sidestepped the steer like a matador. A man behind him was not so lucky, as the steer's horns picked him up and hurled him into the sky. Astonishingly, the man landed on his feet and kept walking, unhurt.

A block away, an entire building had collapsed on a dozen more steers. It was an odd place to find them, but a policeman fired his pistol into a steer to put it out of his misery. The moaning and crying were everywhere. A man cried out, "My leg is gone! My leg is gone!" and Brave Eagle found him on a side street, lying, rolling in agony. A single shredded ligament was all that connected the man's leg below the knee and Brave Eagle withdrew his knife from the satchel and severed the ligament, then tied the man's stump by cutting the arm from his undershirt and wrapping it around.

Brave Eagle followed the fleeing citizens, and made his way to Union Square holding a hand-made poster with a rough illustration of his daughters and the caption "LOST." He expected they would head for the ocean. He would ask at every refugee camp.

A policeman in uniform came up to him.

"We're setting up stations where people can check in for family."

"I have no idea where to start."

"God knows, I hope you find them."

The city was ablaze and the tremors continued every few minutes until another big one at 8:30 proved to be the coup de grace for many buildings that already stood in precarious positions, but collapsed from the final shake. Dogs roamed loose in the streets. Brave Eagle noticed an odd sight: a tree full of yellow canaries. Some people sat on the side of the street, with a pillowcase of possessions. People walked with dazed expressions on their faces. Four men trying to brake a grand piano they rolled down a steep hill.

A man in Union Square suggested, "A lot of people are in tent camps around Fort Mason. There's worry abut a tidal wave; so don't go near the water. Don't go South of Market. Nothing left. Got orders to shoot looters on sight, and they killed a bunch. "

At Powell Street in Union Square a policeman shouted at him: "You. Come with me."

"I have to find my daughters."

"Every able bodied man is needed."

The policeman directed Brave Eagle to a crew removing bricks from the street where a building collapsed. "Here's another man, Stewart!" the policeman shouted, and Brave Eagle spent the rest of the day stacking bricks with a dozen other men. The stench of human decomposition permeated the rubble of bricks, as one body after another was uncovered. Brave Eagle uncovered a crushed infant, only about three months old and then, her parents, together in death.

In the square, one large tent was erected for the police, surrounded by a number of tents and blankets for the dispossessed citizens. These people are like me, after Wounded Knee, Brave Eagle thought. Nothing left but their lives. Some will question whether to go on living. Some will question why God did this. Did He intend for this to happen so they would learn a lesson? Or was He there at all? He never wanted to be in that position again.

Brave Eagle stared at the face of a dead young woman, dried blood emerging from her ear and nose. Her eyes open and her lips curled into a smile. He set to work to uncover the rest of the bricks that crushed her and found a small dog; a tiny poodle had died at her side. He opened her purse and found it belonged to a Sarah Melton, at a Fourth Street address.

"I'll take the purse. Does it have identification?" The crew leader, a policeman asked.

"Yes. She is Sarah Melton of Fourth Street."

"A wealthy young lady from her clothing."

Brave Eagle worked until nightfall. His hands bled from the work. "I need to spend the night somewhere." He told the crew chief.

"Find a spot on the ground tonight. Things are still getting sorted out."

Brave Eagle spent the night under the stars. He used his satchel for a pillow, and put on a blanket he found to keep warm. He moved close to a campfire. Despite the devastation, a man strummed his guitar and several others sang along with him. He fell asleep to the sound of "The Battle Hymn of the Republic." His truth is marching on.

The next morning, he woke at dawn, and followed Powell Street to the Bay. The trolley car lines lay crooked and mangled. He climbed a tremendous hill and from the top, he saw the bay. Then, he descended into Chinatown, where much of the area burnt. The Chinese, tried to reorganize their lives. It reminded him of the reservation, one race in one place. Their area was completely devastated and on fire and he ran down the street to escape the flames that encroached upon the street, holding his breath, the smoke stinging his eyes.

His quadriceps ached from the pounding of walking down the endless hill to the sea. At Columbus Street, a policeman directed him o the refugee camp near Fort Mason.

He went from family to family, showing them the poster of his daughters and finally found success. A young man saw the poster.

"The girls from South Dakota!"

"Are they here?'

"Not any more. Yesterday. The girl pitched baseball. They went off with the baseball team to Oakland."

"She pitched baseball?"

"Yes. The two girls and a boy. She pitched against the San Francisco Seals and they wanted to sign her up and they all went together."

"What did she look like?"

"Like the picture on the poster. Long dark hair. " The man stared at Brave Eagle.

"Indian blood maybe, tans. Like you. And her name was Maka. The younger sister looked like her. But the little boy was blonde headed."

"After the earthquake?"

"Yes. The next day."

Brave Eagle hugged the man. "My daughters."

It took the better part of a day to find a carriage willing to travel to Oakland, and at a majestic price of thirty dollars. Once in Oakland, the next step was to find out where the Seals played, and the carriage took him to the empty baseball stadium.

When nothing was found there, the driver of the carriage dropped Brave Eagle off in downtown Oakland, looking for a hotel that might house the San Francisco Seals, and the eleventh hotel Brave Eagle visited was the right one. The Bayside Hotel desk clerk told him the players were due to check in that afternoon. "Will you tell me when they get here? "

The desk clerk shrugged. "If you are willing to wait."

At six o'clock, several men came into the hotel lobby, one of them carrying a large green duffle bag with San Francisco Seals stenciled. Brave Eagle approached them.

"I was told my daughters were with the San Francisco Seals," he showed them the poster of Maka and Wishiwu.

Rico, the first baseman, took the poster. "Oh yeah, wow. She had a fastball."

"Are they here?"

"No. They said they had to find their parents."

"Where did they go?"

"To Colorado to take the little boy home, they said."

"Where in Colorado?'

"Did they say?" Rico asked the other players.

"Denver," one of them replied.

"Are you sure?"

"I think so."

The search was not over. But, they were alive and survived kidnappers and an earthquake. Throw adversity at them from all sides, God, and they can overcome.

Back to the San Francisco train station went Brave Eagle, again having trouble finding transportation until he threw money at them. At the San Francisco train station, he purchased a ticket to Denver, checked in the Western union office.

A message waited for him.

"Come home. Onashola is in trouble. Betty Pettigrew."

Train rides are for thinking, for looking out the window and watching the terrain change. The train passed over the Sierra Nevada mountain range, where the snow in the mountains melted into Lake Tahoe. Beyond the mountains, nothing but bleak desert. The desert stretched five hundred miles from Reno to Brigham City. Here desolation. There, lushness. He would gather his family together again, and then what? The trip made him think about moving from Rapid City, away from thieves like McEver, away from small-minded people who ran small towns.

Cities were a maze. How do you find someone if you don't have an address? It was a miracle he located someone who saw his daughters. In Rapid City, you walked down the street and everyone knew everyone else.

CHAPTER 9

SHERIFF JAMESON ARRIVED at the height of the fire, as the volunteer fireman sprayed their large hose at the flames. The entire house was ablaze and it was already certain that the house had been completely destroyed, but the location of the house, with the small house occupied by Brave Eagle's family far enough away that it was not threatened by the flames, meant that it would not spread beyond its borders.

He found Betty sitting by a tree, her knees to her chest, covered by a dark brown blanket.

"You OK?" The sheriff knelt down to her level.

"I've mostly lost some memories of my Will. This pretty much seals that chapter of my life. Valuables? Only memories. You can't replace them."

"How did it start?" He sat next to her.

"They threw torches. I heard the glass break, woke up, and the front of the house was on fire. Then a bang at the rear of the house. I crawled out a window and saw a wagon racing away. Towards McEver's of course, but I ran into the town to ring the bell. The house, look at it, too late. If I'd lived closer to town maybe."

"You take a risk living alone like you do."

Betty was silent. "The dog is still barking. We better check next door."

"Onashola never came?"

"No. She had to hear all this shouting and Bone barking. Something's wrong over there."

"You rest here and I will check on her."

As he left her, the firemen wheeled their steam engine away and turned off the hose. One of the men approached Betty.

"Sorry, ma'am. It's too far gone. We'll have to let it burn out. Don't want to risk anyone's lives when the house is a goner."

The Sheriff approached Brave Eagle's house. It was past five a.m. and the flames brightened his walk down the dirt road until he reached the house.

Bone barked and struggle against a hangman's noose tied around his neck and connected to a horse post. He spun in circles as the Sheriff arrived and loosened the noose and let Bone free.

"Good dog, Bone. Where is she?"

He knocked on the door and shouted, "Onashola?" and withdrew his pistol from the holster and opened the door. "Onashola? You here?"

He returned to Betty after searching the house, Bone following him.

"No sign of her."

"We heard from Brave Eagle by wire yesterday that the girls had escaped the men in San Francisco and he was there, looking for them."

'Was Onashola going to go to San Francisco?"

"No. I bet they took her."

"Where?"

"Probably to McEver's. They failed to get the map, so this is what he's doing."

"He can't just take her. I'll go out to the ranch in the morning."

"This is his doing, no doubt."

"Now, now. I know this is a small town, but the laws apply here, too."

"If you go there, bring your deputy. He'll kill you just like he killed my husband."

"I'll be safe. I didn't get this far along without some scrapes. Let's bring you over to Onashola's house. You can stay there."

He pulled her off the ground by the hand and put his arm around her. The flames still shot into the sky and they felt the heat on their faces as the sound of collapsing wood continued and half of the town watched.

Jameson found a lamp and lit it as they sat on a table that faced Betty's burning house some hundred yards away.

"My husband's dream. There it goes." Tears filled her eyes.

"You can rebuild if you want. Don't you still own the other house?"

"No. I deeded this to Brave Eagle and Onashola. Will said he felt destiny drew him and me to Rapid City. I may as well carry it out. God knows. I've lost him, the house, and the children, all for gold. Why do I stay and not go back to Massachusetts?"

"It's hard in times like this if people say, I know how you feel because they don't. All I can say is when I lost my wife, I felt like I had lost everything, too, but I keep on. I don't believe in this destiny stuff like your late husband. I just am a lawman, that's my calling. Someone has to do it. It'll be me that goes out and figures out what McEver is up to. If he did it, and he probably had his men do it, why would he? Knowing him, it will probably be that he says some wild Indians are on the loose. He might even blame Onashola, which could be an excuse. She burned your house down and ran away."

Jameson reached out and held her hand.

"I'm very sorry about your house."

"It was nice, but what is it after all. Nothing but four walls to keep you from the cold. Brave Eagle and Onashola spent most of their lives living in little tipis and they say this little house here is a luxury to them. The only thing valuable in there was memories, photographs and papers."

Jameson grew quiet as more tears flowed from her eyes. She reminded him somewhat of his wife, Linda. Betty and Linda were both strong women who faced adversity and didn't blink an eye. He knew it had been difficult being married to a lawman, because many times he left the house for an emergency and who knew if he would return alive.

Lawrence and Kansas City had their share of excitement. In his career, he had seen six of the men he convicted hanged. And all six he felt sorry for at the end. The worst was old Billy Brackett, who was convicted of killing his wife by hitting her in the head with a shovel. His defense was that she was an evil woman who poisoned his dog. The dog, indeed, was dead. Billy told him, "You'd a killed her, too, if you was me."

"Killing a dog is not the same as killing a person."

"It oughta be. That dog meant more to me than she did and she knew it so she killed him and I killed her. If I have to go to Hell for the rest of my life, I don't care, because she deserved it."

Throughout the west, law was complicated by either crooked sheriffs and crooked judges and Jameson's biggest problem in Rapid City was the judge. Anything to do with men employed by McEver and they were let off lightly. He knew Judge Secrist was under McEver's thumb and that would complicate his investigation.

Betty put her head down and Jameson discovered he was stroking her hair to soothe her. It seemed like a natural reaction. He considered her an attractive woman, one of those natural beauties that did not have to resort to heavy makeup and perfume. He guessed he was at least ten years older than her, maybe twelve or so. It suddenly struck upon him the idea that maybe he would court her when this was all settled and if she didn't leave. Courting was something he had only done once in his life and that was thirty years before.

He could help her build the house. She was alone. He was alone. Perhaps? Would they make each other happy? Well, now was not the time to pursue that course. Betty cried quietly into her arms, her head still on the table, when Jameson leaned down and kissed the back of her head. She stopped crying at that, and held her breath, but did not raise her head.

Onashola groggily put her feet on the floor, but grew dizzy at the effort and returned to the cot and lay back. After a few minutes, the fog in her brain began to clear. She was in a small cabin. To her right were a fireplace and a pine table and two chairs.

The cot faced the door and above her head, a window. There was a second window on the opposite wall. Two pair of muddy cowboy boots were by the front door and a man's duster coat and hat hung from a hook.

She had no idea where she was. The fire! She pulled herself out of the cot and stood by the window. It drizzled outside, a dreary day on some sort of farm. She saw a fence with several horses drinking from a trough and through the opposite window saw McEver's house. It all made sense. McEver's men burned Mrs. Pettigrew's house and took her. He's holding me hostage for the stupid map, she thought.

The fireplace had an iron stoker beneath some logs. How convenient, they left me a weapon, she thought. Onashola went to the door, but it was locked from the outside. Taking a few steps made her dizzy again and she returned to the cot.

A weapon. Horses nearby. It only took her a minute to plan out her escape. A wave of nausea came over her and she leaned over and vomited on the floor. She was in no shape to escape at the moment. They must have drugged her and she fell back asleep.

The door opened several hours later, and one of the ranch hands looked in on her as she returned to consciousness. He was a grungy man, his face and beard reddened from the wind and sprinkled with mud, wearing leather jodhpurs caked in mud. He took off his wet coat and changed into the dry coat.

"The boss wants to see you. It's fun time," the man said, not looking at her. His gun was holstered, and he sat on the chair, pulling off his muddy boots only to replace them with even muddier boots by the door.

"Why am I here?"

"Well, I think you are to be traded for something," the cowboy said. The cowboy smelled of mildew all the way across the room. Did these men ever bathe? He spied the poker in the fireplace and got up from the chair and took it.

"You won't be needing a fire. It's warm enough. Come with me. Don't try to run." He pulled his Colt from the holster and directed her to the ranch house. She was barefoot and in her nightshirt, and as she walked, the mud squished beneath her toes.

Onashola was led into a huge bedroom where McEver sat on a leather sofa across from the bed. The room had mirrors everywhere. A large mirror overlooked a chest of drawers on the left side of the bed. Above the bed was a mirror on the ceiling.

"Tie her so she can't get loose. These people have a knack for getting untied," McEver instructed. He smoked a cigar and was dressed in a velvet robe and slippers, ready for bed. The cowboy tied Onashola to the chair, like roping a calf and she gave a momentary tug against the coiled rope and realized there was no escaping.

"Some entertainment for you, Onashola. Show them in."

The cowboy opened the door and Jenkins led McEver's blindfolded wife into the room. She was dressed in a sheer black nightgown and her hands tied and they led her to the bed.

"Lie down," Jenkins demanded.

He took off her nightgown so she was naked and lay on her stomach and the two men tied her hands to the bedposts. Then, they took strips of sheet and tied her feet to the bed, splayed in front of them, her legs and arms spread wide apart.

Jenkins sat atop her, while the cowboy undressed.

"Ride me, pretty horsey."

She began to writhe up and down while the man rode her like a horse, putting his hands between her legs and massaging her thighs.

"Doesn't take you long to get wet, sweetheart?"

"No. No. I want you both at the same time."

Onashola shut her eyes.

"Oh no, Onashola. You are next!" McEver ordered. With his fingers, he pried her eyes open.

"Honey, show her what you can do!"

Onashola turned her face away, but McEver twisted it back.

"You are going to like it here, Indian girl. Very much."

"Stop this! You re sick!"

"Bart, put something in her mouth."

The cowboy came over, naked and erect and stuffed a stocking in Onashola's mouth.

The rope was bound tight around her and she tried to withdraw her shoulders so she might slither out of the rope, but she couldn't budge. She tipped the chair and it crashed to the floor.

"Oh, you are no fun. You should watch, so you know what do when it is your turn. Okay, Bart, do her now, and honey, tell him how much you like it. "

Onashola lay on the floor, listening to the grunts of the men and the woman and the creaking of the bed, when another man entered the room.

"Mr. McEver. A message. It's important."

McEver took the message. "Go away, Tim."

McEver opened the envelope and read the message.

"Uh oh. Of all the places on earth!"

He leered down at Onashola and spoke into her face.

"An earthquake in San Francisco. I lost a hotel, Goddamn it!" McEver stormed out of the room, angry.

How did McEver know where her daughters were unless he intercepted telegrams?

Onashola lay on the ground, tied to the chair, twisting again to loosen the binds, to no avail. There were some final spurts of enthusiasm from the bed above her, and the men came off the bed and untied McEver's wife.

From her vantage point on the floor, Onashola saw Jenkins slap Mrs. McEver on the ass as she left the room, laughing. He came over to her and struggled with the rope. "Damn, Bart. Untie this!"

The cowboy, wearing his long underclothes, untied the rope. "You want to do her, too?"

"No, The boss left. He would get mad if he couldn't watch. Tomorrow maybe."

There would be no tomorrow, Onashola vowed as the cowboy untied her. He led her back to the cabin, holding his gun to her back. As he shoved her into the cabin, she saw the poker lying by the front door where the man dropped it. But he locked the door.

About two o'clock in the morning, she took a log from the fireplace and threw it through the window, shielding herself from the
glass shards with the cowboy's coat and eased out the window. She
hit the ground running and the cowboy yelled out, "Hey! I'll shoot!"

She grabbed the poker and as the cowboy turned the corner of the
cabin, slammed it into his stomach. The man screamed and fell to the
ground, dropping his pistol, which Onashola scooped up and ran for the
horse stable. The stable was unguarded and she mounted a horse and was
free as shouts rang out from the house.

Onashola rode the horse down the road, guided by the moonlight,
when she heard the engine of an automobile. A motorcar! She steered
her horse off the road, into a clump of trees. The lights of the automobile
came into view and passed.

She took a back road around the town. While McEver searched Rapid
City, she was on the way to the Pine Ridge reservation. McEver did not
dare go to the reservation.

The next morning, Jameson paid another visit to Leo McEver. Jenkins
brought him into the office, where McEver who already appeared agi-
tated over a stack of papers on his desk, peered above his glasses.

"What's your business, Sheriff?"

"Two things, Mister McEver. A wagon was seen leaving the scene
of the Pettigrew house fire and headed in your direction. And seeing as
there is nothing after your ranch until North Dakota, I figured it's one of
your hands again."

"You get a description?"

"No, but I want to talk to your men."

"They are all out working now, so come back at six. Be my guest. I
don't know anything about it. What they do on their own time I have
nothing to do with."

"You heard about the fire?"

"Yes. Some of my men don't live on the ranch and saw the house on
the way here."

"The other thing is Onashola Heard came up missing." Jameson sat back in his stool, eager for an explanation.

"What did she do? Go to find her husband?"

"She just disappeared."

"Well, I don't know anything about Onashola. I haven't seen her."

"Here is what I know, Mister McEver. Brave Eagle is in San Francisco and so are they. At least they were there before the earthquake. He hasn't found them."

"There were thousands killed in San Francisco. I lost my best hotel."

"Quite a tragedy."

"So, she's probably gone to San Francisco to find them."

"She didn't ride a stage and didn't take her own carriage. From what I can see, she would have to walk."

"How do you know somebody else didn't give her a ride somewhere?"

"She would have told Betty Pettigrew if she was going somewhere."

"I told you, I don't know anything about her. Jenkins, you can show the Sheriff around the ranch. She's not here."

Jenkins motioned to Jameson, "Come on. I'll show you."

Jameson returned to Rapid City and found Betty sitting on Brave Eagle's front porch in a rocking chair.

"I doubted you would open the library today."

"I know it's supposed to be open today, but I spent the morning sifting through the ashes."

"Find anything?"

"A few odds and ends."

"Mind if I join you?"

She motioned to the empty chair next to hers and he slid into Brave Eagle's rocker. He rocked silently before saying a word and finally muttered, "Guess this is what retirement will be like. Rocking in a chair, looking at the road."

"Who's retiring?"

"I will some day. Hope to do that before I get killed on the job."

"What will you do then?"

"Tucson. I have a sister there. Been there twice. Except for the hot summers, it's great. Beautiful place."

"I've never been there. When will this be?'

"Six, seven years. Like I said, if I don't get killed first. I've had enough narrow scrapes for one lifetime."

"What was the worst?"

"It was not even a skirmish. I walked underneath a tree in Kansas City and a man was cutting branches with long scissors and he dropped them and the blades came right down towards me and just missed my head, but landed in the back of my shirt. The scissors were sticking out of my back and at first I thought they were in my back but I did not feel any pain. That was only an inch from my head and that would have been it."

"Ever been in a shootout?"

"Oh several. The one time in Kansas was one of those with the man out in the street, calling me out: Draw! And I said, 'Don't do it!' But he went for it, and I hit the ground and he was way off, but I got him with one shot. Didn't kill him, but got him in his shooting shoulder. He dropped the gun and when he went to pick it up, I got him right in his hand and he was screaming and that was over. That man got the hangman's noose, eventually."

"I don't believe in hanging. Except maybe I could see hanging McEver. Such a vile man."

"You mean evil?"

"Evil, vile, putrid, ugly. He's all that. "

"There's one of him in every town, and more than one in every city. I guess God created evilness same as goodness, maybe to show us up front what it looks like."

"I don't think God created McEver or evilness."

"Think not?"

"Want some biscuits and honey?"

"Sure. Did Onashola have food in the house?"

"I made the biscuits this morning and coffee. Want some?"

"That'd be nice."

Betty retreated into the house, while Jameson rocked. It was a pleasant April day, maybe the first morning one could sit outside on a porch and watch the world go by.

She returned and passed him a plate of two buttermilk biscuits with a spoon dipped in honey and a mug of steaming coffee.

"Ah, I would say this is the life, but considering you're here, and over there is your burned down house, it isn't exactly the right thing to say."

"I know what you mean, though. I could live in a house like this. My husband thought we would be having a big family, eventually."

"And you never remarried, a woman as attractive as you must have had many suitors."

Oh, I'm beyond that. Once a woman hits fifty, they put you out to pasture like an old horse."

"No one ever courted you in all the time since your husband died?'

"Not a one, but I don't exactly put out an interest in another man."

"Oh." McEver figured that was meant to discourage him if that was where he was headed.

"And you? You ever think of marrying again?"

"Same thing. I'm past sixty now. Used to be, when I was younger, if I walked down the street, I'd look at women to smile at them and they'd smile back. Now they don't see me any more. They look right through me. Old man. Unless they notice my badge. Then they smile sometimes. But I'm fine, living above the jailhouse. I don't need much more than a bed to lay my tired bones on."

"That's something we have in common," Betty observed, holding her coffee mug tightly, "a widow and a widower, making the best of what they got left."

"Amen!"

Maka, Wishiwu, and their newfound friend, Bobby got off the train in Denver, an address in hand on the eighteen hundred block of Elmwood, which Bobby remembered as being near Cherry Creek Park. It was late in the morning, and the girls noticed the thin, dry air.

"I suppose we'll stay until we locate your aunt and uncle," Maka suggested. "Are you friends with any neighbors?"

'My friend Larry lives down the street. His mother can help."

They rented a carriage outside the train station to take them to Bobby's home address. He proved to be a talkative little chap on the train ride.

"Who was this Caruso fellow?"

"Oh, my parents listen to opera and he was their favorite singer."

"They took you?"

"He was loud but sounded good. Maka?"

"Yes?"

"I don't want to go with my aunt. Can I go with you and Wishiwu?"

"Is something wrong with your aunt and uncle?"

"Yes."

"What? Do they hurt you?"

"You'll see."

"What?"

"See for yourself."

When they got to the house, Bobby knew of a spare key beneath a bush. The house was a modest red brick bungalow, with a front porch. They opened the door and it was cold inside.

"We need to heat this place!" Wishiwu said.

"There's a fireplace and a coal furnace, but I don't know how it works."

"I don't either, but we can light a fire in the fireplace."

The living room had a wooden coffee table and two sitting chairs. On the mantle were pictures of the family - a photo of the mother and father, with a three-year old version of Bobby. Bobby lowered his eyes. He folded his arms and sat back into the chair, trying to hold back the tears, but he couldn't because there were reminders of his parents everywhere. His mother's books on the coffee table. His father's war medal from the Spanish-American War hung on the wall. A painting of Ames, Iowa, his mother's hometown.

"A nice house. Much bigger than ours. Let's look round," Wishiwu suggested.

The house had two bedrooms and a bathroom with a tub.

"Is there hot water," Maka insisted, and Wishiwu turned on the water. "Ah! Yes! Me first!"

While Wishiwu took a bath, Maka searched the kitchen cabinets for food. She found a bag of rice, a box of oatmeal, and some stale crackers. Not much. She poured some rice into a tin pot and boiled water on the gas stove.

Wishiwu came back from the tub, and they sat down at the kitchen table to eat the rice.

"I have an idea," Wishiwu offered. "Maka, we are Bobby's aunts. We stay, and get momma and poppa to move here. You should say you are older than eighteen. Like twenty."

"You could be my aunts!" Bobby shouted with glee.

They created life histories. Maka and Wishiwu were to be the sisters of their mother, and they had gone with them to San Francisco."

"So your aunt that lives here is the sister of your father?" Maka asked. "Yes."

"Has she ever met your mother's family from Iowa?"

"I don't know."

"Does your mother have family in Iowa?"

"My grandparents."

"Where are your other grandparents?"

"My father's parents are dead."

"We should take you to Iowa," Maka suggested. "It is a little closer to South Dakota."

"I want to stay with you, wherever you go."

"Let's do that," Wishiwu said. "I want him to be our little brother now."

Maka found some paper and envelopes, and wrote a letter to their parents with the address in Denver.

"Dear Momma and Poppa,

We were in the earthquake, but not hurt, and made it out thanks to a baseball team. We found a little boy whose parents had been killed and he lived in Denver. So we decided to take him to his house. We took the train here and are staying in his house. Please come here.

We will stay here until we hear from you. The address is 1853 Elmwood in Denver. We love you, signed, Maka and Wishiwu."

Maka sealed the letter and asked Bobby, "Where is the post office?"

"I don't know."

"We'll ask the neighbors. This time I'm taking it to the post office myself. Let's go see Larry's parents."

They walked a few doors down.

"Act older," Wishiwu whispered as they knocked on the door. Wishiwu held Bobby's hand. "Remember, we are your aunts from Iowa. What are your grandma and grandpa's names?"

"Grandpa Bailey and Grandma Bailey."

"No. I mean their first names. We are supposed to be their daughters."

"I don't know."

"Didn't your mother ever call them something else besides Grandma and Grandpa?"

"No."

Maka grimaced. "Let's hope nobody asks us about our parents in Iowa. We'll call them Momma and Poppa."

That afternoon, they found the post office and mailed the letter, and knocked on the door of Bobby's neighborhood friend, Larry.

A woman came to the door, wearing a white apron. She was in her thirties, thin, with dashes of flour in her curly hair. She slapped her hands on the apron, causing a puff of flour and got down on her knees.

"Oh, Bobby! Bobby! You are not hurt!"

She hugged him close to her, and her son, Larry appeared behind her.

"Bobby!"

"Your parents?" She looked up at Maka and Wishiwu and they shook their heads.

"Died," Maka said, and Bobby cried in the woman's arms.

"You are?"

"We are Bobby's aunts from Iowa." Maka asked.

"She never mentioned sisters."

"We are step-sisters," Wishiwu intervened.

"You were with them?"

"Yes. The bricks from our hotel fell on them when we ran out of the hotel."

Larry's mother was concerned. "The Denver papers should be told. They would want to print an obituary. Bobby's father was quite prominent in the attorney general's office."

"Oh. We don't know how to do that."

"How old are you?"

"Eighteen, Wishiwu is fifteen," Maka said.

"Wishiwu. What an unusual name. Your name?"

"Maka."

"My name is Mary Gray. Well, I should help you. Are your parents going to come here?"

"They don't know we are alive."

"Oh, my. Let me help."

"No, that's okay," Maka said. "We can take care of it."

"Do you want me to notify the newspaper?"

"Yes, but we didn't know Bobby's father well, and haven't even seen his mother in years, so I don't know what to put in a newspaper."

"Oh, you tell about the things they did in life."

"Why don't you put that they died," Wishiwu said.

"You can't leave things like that."

"We have to go back to the house now."

"All right. I'll be over in an hour."

Maka and Wishiwu returned to Bobby's house.

"I think she knows we are not aunts," Wishiwu said.

"Well, what made you say step-sisters?"

"To throw her off the course."

"Well, don't make it worse." They went into the house, and Maka found a photograph album with labeled pictures. "Her parents were Mr. and Mrs. Charles and Estelle Bailey. Now we explain why we don't know anything about them."

"Should we tell her the truth?"

"I like this little boy," she patted Bobby's head. "I'm afraid he will end out in an orphanage."

"Do you think Momma and Poppa would care for him?"

"They would, if they met him."

"Why don't we say we are the bastard children of Mr. Bailey instead of his step-daughters?" Wishiwu suggested.

"Oh, come on. Make the lie as big as you can. Let's see if Bobby's mother is thirty and I am twenty and they never divorced, how could they even have a stepsister? She will figure it out. I have a better idea. We are cousins and lied about being aunts because we are afraid they will take him away. We are cousins from...Bobby did your grandpa or grandma have brothers and sisters?"

"I don't know."

"Well, if Bobby doesn't, nobody else does."

"What are we going to do when the grandpa and grandma come?"

"They'll want to take him with them, most likely. But we can ask if we keep him. Do you go to school, Bobby?"

"Not yet."

"Good. You'll probably start first grade next year. We must think this through."

By the time Mary Gray arrived at the house, Maka found an address book with the address of the grandparents and the aunt that lived in Denver. She sat down and began taking notes.

As she took notes, Maka interjected:

"Mrs. Gray. We can't tell a lie. We are not related to Bobby at all. We found him in the earthquake by his parents and brought him here. We are afraid they are going to put Bobby in an orphanage so we told you a story. If Bobby's grandparents don't take him, we want to take him to our parents."

Mrs. Gray nodded. "I understand. But I think the grandparents will have to agree."

Maka wrote to Bobby's grandparents:

Dear Mr. and Mrs. Bailey,

I am sorry to inform you your daughter and her husband were killed in the San Francisco earthquake, but Bobby is fine. We took a train back to his home in Denver.

If you don't think you can take Bobby, I am sure my parents will. My name is Maka. We are in the Denver house, and will await your letter. Sincerely, Maka Heard

Mrs. Gray contacted Bobby's father's employer and the local aunt the next day.

"What's wrong with her?" Maka asked him.

"She's evil, my dad said. And she hits me every time. One time she said Bobby get me the mug and I didn't do it right away and she slapped me in the face. I called her mean and she washed my mouth out with soap!"

"Where were your parents?"

"They went to the opera that night and she came over while they were gone."

The next day, the word spread in the neighborhood about Bobby's parents and a swarm of neighbors brought over food and baked goods. Maka and Wishiwu survived the barrage of questions hurled at them and beheld a table full of cakes, pies, and casseroles.

"There's enough food for a week here," Wishiwu said.

"That's about the time Momma and Poppa will get our letter. Where are they? Can you imagine? We've been gone three weeks now and they must be going crazy. First, we disappear, we let them know we went to San Francisco and it falls into the sea, and they must think we are dead until they get our letter."

"It makes me want to get a telephone. But the only phone I know of is the sheriff in Rapid City and we better not call him," Wishiwu added.

"It would make things a lot easier, if everybody had a phone in their own house."

Maka and Wishiwu did figure it would take a week for their parents and Bobby's grandparents to get their letters. While they waited, neighbors continued to bring food and Maka and Wishiwu became more and more attached to Bobby.

Bobby proved to be super intelligent. Although he was not yet in school, he could read and had a collection of books. Maka picked out A Tale of Two Cities to read, while Wishiwu read Huckleberry Finn. They remarked how well he would fit into their family of readers.

For entertainment, they played checkers. Bobby taught them how to play chess and proceeded to beat both sisters. Maka observed, "I never was good at thinking two moves ahead!"

There was schoolhouse two blocks away, the one Bobby would be attending the next September, with a yard, and after the schoolchildren left, Maka and Wishiwu ran circles around the field, teaching Bobby running was exhilarating and fun. They played "Tag" and "Kick the Can."

One day, Mary Gray, after discovering the girls liked reading, took them to a new store in Denver that sold nothing but books. She bought "The Count of Monte Cristo," for Maka and "The Wonderful Wizard of Oz," for Wishiwu.

Maka lit the fireplace after Bobby went to bed.

"I want to keep him, Wishiwu." Maka said.

"Me, too."

"The grandparents will take him."

"Maybe not. Maybe they will be too old and not want to take him."

"If they take him back to Iowa, we could always ask momma and poppa to move there, too. We could move down the street from him," Wishiwu offered.

"In some ways, I wish we ran away with our parents and live somewhere with no memory of South Dakota, like Alaska."

"It's cold enough in South Dakota for me," Wishiwu said. "I don't want to live with the Eskimo and walruses."

"Even Florida. Doesn't matter. Why did our lives change? All over a map! Ruin our lives. "

The next day at eight o'clock in the morning, a knock at the front door and there stood Bobby's aunt and uncle. The woman was forty but appeared sixty, with dark circles and heavy sagging skin under her eyes, and hair that sat on her head like a wet, disheveled mop. She wore what appeared to be a dead fox wrapped around her neck, with the head of the fox still attached. The husband was a giant of a man, about 6 feet six and two hundred eighty pounds. He wore a three-piece suit, but his stomach was so large, the vest buttons opened to give the stomach breathing room and had a large mustache, and Maka thought he resembled Chester Arthur, the former President.

"Hello, I am Bobby's Aunt Gladys and this is Uncle Rolly. We've come for Bobby."

"Oh, my," Maka said. "His grandparents are coming from Iowa."

"All right. We can take him for now and when they come we will make some arrangements with them."

"He's asleep, but we can't let you take him until the grandparents come," Maka insisted.

"Let us in" Aunt Gladys demanded.

Maka opened the door wider and the couple came into the house.

Aunt Gladys had a smoker's hacking coughing fit and bought tears to her eyes before she recovered.

"Where is he?"

"Asleep in his room."

"Wake him up!"

"No. We'll let him sleep," Maka argued.

"Who are you?" Aunt Gladys protested. "Get him."

"We are his cousins from Iowa and waiting for his grandmother."

"Do I get him myself? We rented the carriage for the day and paid fifteen dollars. We're bringing him back with us and you can send the grandparents to hash it out with us!"

"He's going to Iowa."

"Do I get the Police?"

"His father worked for the Governor. Do I get the Governor?"

"Yeah!" added Wishiwu, enthused by her sister's stubbornness.

"What room is he in? I'll get him myself!"

The woman made a move to the bedroom and Maka grabbed her by the arm.

"He's not going!"

"Now you lay your hands off my wife!" the big man protested.

"I'm getting him!"

She tried to twist free, but Maka held firm.

"Rolly!" the woman shouted. "Do something!"

"I will get him!"

The man shoved Maka and Wishiwu aside and went into Bobby's bedroom, where he sat in his nightshirt, wiping the sleep from his eyes.

"Come on! Bobby!" The man picked him up and as he turned to walk away, Maka leapt into the air and kicked him square in the face with such force all two hundred eighty pounds fell backwards to the bed, breaking the frame of the bed and sending the mattress to the floor. A geyser of blood spouted from Uncle Rolly's nose.

"What have you done?" Aunt Gladys screamed. "I'm calling the police! You are going to jail, you little tramp!"

"You can't take him!" Maka yelled. "Get out of here! I'll kick the snot right out of your nose!"

"You little bitch! Rolly, come on, we'll have them arrested."

She extended her hand to help her husband up, but he waved her off and got up on his own, holding his nose, which continued to spurt blood.

"We'll be back with the police!" Aunt Gladys said.

"Don't call them, Auntie! Please!" Bobby begged. "I don't want to go with you!"

"We're your family. Not them!"

Aunt Gladys and Rolly returned to the one-horse carriage and rode away.

"What do we do now? Do we run?" Wishiwu asked her sister.

'We ought to leave. I don't know what to do."

CHAPTER 10

⚜

ONASHOLA HAD NOT set foot on the Pine Ridge Reservation since Brave Eagle carried her away from the Episcopalian Mission. The most notable difference was people now lived in houses. A few tipis remained as she approached the center of the reservation, but mostly, the tribe adopted four walls as a mode of living.

The Mayor's office was located in the center of the reservation in a nondescript white adobe two-bedroom house converted into offices. The Mayor's secretary glanced up from typing as Onashola stepped into the office.

"Hello?" she asked. She was a young, twenty years old, girl, dressed in a blouse with a turquoise necklace. She peered from over the lens of her glasses.

"My name is Onashola. I am in need of a place to stay. I am not sure who lives here any more. Does Black Elk still live here?"

The secretary pushed her glasses higher on her nose. "Yes, he does. Oglala?"

"Yes."

"Onashola. Were you at Wounded Knee?"

"Yes."

"The one with the baby?"

"That's me."

The woman rose from her chair and took Onashola's hand. "Everyone always wondered what happened to you. We heard you left with Brave Eagle. The story is of legend now. Tell me. Where did you go?"

"Brave Eagle and I moved to Rapid City and married. We have two daughters."

"So a happy ending. Wonderful!"

"Well, not entirely. We have trouble in Rapid City and that is why I need help."

"What kind of trouble?"

"I won't bother you with that now."

"I live with my mother and my sister got married, so we have an extra bed. Its pretty bare, our house, but we have electricity. The Mayor got a telephone, so things are improving here."

'Oh, that would help."

"My name is Dancing Deer. I get off work at five, so if you want to wait on the bench, you can come home with me."

Onashola sat in front of a board that posted events for the community. Someone was selling a sewing machine. Another posted an ad for free puppies. She read through a list of the Reservation officers. Not one was a name she recognized. Indians came into the office with various needs, and Dancing Deer jotted down their information. A man came in claiming his neighbor ate one of his chickens, and Dancing Deer registered the complaint. A man wanted to use the telephone to call the Great White Father in Washington D.C. and complain about alcohol.

"I am not sure of why you want the President?"

"My son beats his wife."

Onashola listened to their complaints until she went home with Dancing Deer. In the next week, she would tell the story of her daughters' kidnapping and her own abduction a dozen times, with a growing and interested audience.

Sheriff Jameson took up almost daily residence with Betty Pettigrew, checking on her for several hours every day. His daily routine included a walk through the town streets, looking in at the library, which Betty had yet to re-open, followed by a visit with her that lasted through lunch. He returned to the jailhouse while his deputy took a shift and the Sheriff napped in his own bed for an hour. At precisely six, he re-visited Betty and they had supper together. He would stay until sunset.

One afternoon, he was handed an envelope labeled "Sheriff Jameson."

He read the note and took it directly to Betty's house.

"Onashola is in Pine Ridge," he announced. Betty sat on the front porch, knitting and Sheriff sat besides her. Bone raised his head to see who had invaded the porch, wagged his tail twice, and returned to sleep.

They were quiet awhile.

"I hope I'm not overstaying my welcome," he commented.

"It's mighty good of you to watch over me, but I am fine now. This is good news. So McEver's men took her to his ranch and she escaped. Isn't that a crime? Can't you put him in jail for that?'

"I'll need the district attorney from Sioux City to issue a warrant, only if Onashola herself makes a formal complaint. The law in South Dakota makes Kansas look good."

"The west is just lawless. It's not like Massachusetts."

"What keeps you from going back?"

"The open spaces. There's something beautiful in this prairie earth. My husband once said it was the first time he felt at home, at peace. I feel the same way. It wasn't lonely to him. Is it lonely for you since your wife died?"

"She's still with me, in my heart."

"And my husband with me. I feel he started something and I should see it through."

"What surprises me is your husband was another one of those after gold. Most of them are fools who don't know a lick about mining, thought it was easy. It isn't."

"Yes it was for gold, but if not for gold, he would have sought something else. My husband was a dreamer. And he wanted to do things himself instead of relying on other people to do it for him."

"But this burning down your house due to that madman, doesn't that change things?"

"There are McEver's in every town, in every city. He's a character right out of Dickens. And if you give in, they win. That is all they want.

He's from Massachusetts, too, not South Dakota. Hardly anyone is from here, except Brave Eagle and Onashola. Did you know Brave Eagle killed Custer and our lives are all entangled around Custer?"

"I thought it was Crazy Horse."

"No, it was really Brave Eagle. And Onashola's father was killed at Little Big Horn. He was a soldier. It was entirely possible Brave Eagle killed Onashola's father without knowing it. And we, we're here because Custer told everyone about the gold in the Black Hills. Golden hair. Golden hills. Men would be happy flattening them to the ground in search of riches. It's something hard to understand about mankind in general. They would destroy beauty for a dollar. And our own laws. Why is it not that the Indians lease the land?"

"They live nomadic lives, moving to follow the buffalo. We're used to having a plot of land, a house and a horse and never moving, unless we have to. For me, all's I need are four walls and a bed and a way to eat. I'm simple."

"No. That man is wrong if he thinks burning my house down will get him his gold."

It was early on a Friday evening; an almost summery feel the total devastation of the Pettigrew Georgian mansion singed Brave Eagle's nostrils. He smelled the fire. His house next door was untouched and as Brave Eagle quickened his step to his own front door, Bone rose from the porch and his tail wagged with glee at the sight of his master.

"Old Bone. Always here. Such a good boy!" Brave Eagle kneeled down to pet his old friend, who was at least sixteen years old. Bone emitted a tiny whine as Brave Eagle patted his head. The dog turned his head so he licked the salty sweat from the back of Brave Eagle's hand. Finally, Brave Eagle stood.

"Let's go inside."

The door was locked, so he knocked on the door, and peered through the glass. Betty Pettigrew approached the door. Her arms rose with joy when she saw Brave Eagle and she unlocked the bolted door.

"You've made it back! Oh, thank God!"

They hugged, and Betty cried with relief.

"What happened?"

"Come, sit down. First, everyone is all right. Sit down."

They sat on the sofa in the living room, and Bone curled up at his master's feet.

"Onashola went to Pine Ridge for safety. The night of the fire. A carriage rode away and she was gone. Today, I got this note McEver's men took her but she got away and went to Pine Ridge and you would find her there. This came today."

She handed him an envelope and he recognized Maka's handwriting with a Denver return address. He tore it open and read.

"Safe in Denver!" He dropped the letter to his lap.

"You might be interested in this." He lifted up the satchel from the floor, and withdrew the sheath of papers. He found the deed and handed it to her.

She pulled her reading glasses to her eyes and read through it.

"It seems odd, doesn't it, you never knew? McEver has been on your land! My guess is he can't find any more gold."

Betty leans back on the sofa. "What will you do now?"

"I am not leaving without Onashola. I will get her in Pine Ridge, then head for Denver.

Brave Eagle nodded. "All this time, I'm surprised no one, some clerk or something, never pointed it out."

"My husband didn't care. We had enough money to last four lifetimes, so why get greedy?"

"You should get a lawyer."

"For that, I need to go to Sioux Falls. Tell me about San Francisco."

"Destroyed. They enlisted me to help. Something drew me to a certain park. In my heart, I knew without any doubt, even a quake could not harm them. If a building fell down upon them, the bricks would miss them. I knew it in my bones. When I went to this park and asked around, a man recognized her and why? Because she played in a baseball game and the team gave them a ride to the train station. Again, I stopped at Western Union where I got your message."

"Now, you have an address where they are."

Brave Eagle stood and walked to the window that faced Betty's house. "Will you rebuild?"

"I hope it is all right to stay with you until they do. Yes. This is where we put down roots."

"Why not leave? I think about it myself. When I saw the great city of San Francisco, I wanted to live there. A beautiful city on the ocean. Not one person asked me if I was an Indian. I blended in, but now it is gone. I will discuss with Onashola, because all this tragedy...it is as if South Dakota is cursed!"

"And this is the map that caused so much trouble?' Betty withdrew the piece of parchment from the papers, looked it over and took it to the stove. She opened the latch and threw the paper inside and watched it ignite.

"There. It is done."

So, that night, for the first night in many moons, Brave Eagle slept in his own bed. He woke the next morning, boiled a cup of coffee and took his tin mug out to the front porch. A bird sang a pleasant, lilting song and he sat down in the rocking chair for a moment of peace.

Bone was curled up next to the chair, but he did not, as usual, sit up for a pet from Brave Eagle.

Brave Eagle looked at Bone. "Bone?"

He reached down and touched him and the dog's cold body. "Bone!"

He got down on his knees and lifted the dog's lifeless head.

Brave Eagle put his head on the dog's body and wept from the depths of his being.

Not far from this porch, by the library, was where he found the young stray. The dog had been his friend through tragedy and joy.

He stroked Bone's fur. They experienced so much together. Bone represented the beginning of his family, the first one to help him build something out of nothing. He told Bone they would meet again and thanked God for giving him the time they spent together. Bone proved to be a playmate to his daughters, chasing balls, running through the fields. They would be heartbroken at the news. He sat for a good hour, when Betty walked to the porch, prepared to go to the bank and saw Brave Eagle petting Bone.

"Bone passed in the night."

"Oh, I'm so sorry!" She knelt by the dog.

"I remember when you found him. Who'd have thought a 3-legged dog would live so long! He must be close to twenty. The whole town of Rapid City is going to be sad about this. Some people called him, "The Mayor," because he was always around. I'm really sorry, Brave Eagle. But I did notice he hardly was awake at all while you were gone. It's like he stayed alive just long enough to see you. Just like Argos, the dog of Ulysses."

"I remember that story. Only I am not disguised as a beggar and have to string a bow to claim my wife."

"I'm going to sign over the deed this morning, to the Sioux. I should have done that years ago!"

"That's the way it should be, thought they are not going to go out and try to find a gold mine there. It keeps the land out of the wrong hands."

Brave Eagle wrapped his dog in a blanket and carried him to a spot at the edge of the property, near some trees where Bone rested on hot summer's days. He took a spade and dug a hole where he placed his friend of so many years. Brave Eagle crossed himself. He finished his task and sat by the grave. He considered how that would be a good place for himself to be buried.

Not long after the thought came into his mind, of getting away, a car stopped at his house and a man came out, with the engine still running and went to the front door. After a while, the man walked to the rear of the house, and peered into a window seeing nobody, he walked out to the barn. Brave eagle lay flat to the ground behind a discarded old wagon wheel, where he could observe the man. It was one of McEver's men, to be sure, who else had a motorcar in Rapid City? Nobody.

The next day, Brave Eagle set out in a carriage for Pine Ridge. He arrived that afternoon and after asking around, arrived at Dancing Deer's house. Dancing Deer came to the door and smiled.

"Brave Eagle's here!' she shouted to the back of the house.

"I'm Dancing Deer, Brave Eagle. I am glad you are here!"

Onashola beamed with delight at the sight of her husband. She wore a buckskin dress Dancing Deer loaned her. To Brave Eagle, she appeared no older than the day they married. She wrapped her arms around him, and cried joyful tears. They hugged without moving for a long time.

"You two have a lot to talk about," Dancing Deer suggested. "I'll go for a walk and leave you alone."

Onashola took Brave Eagle by the hand and walked him back to the only bedroom in the house, with two beds and a nightstand, decorated with a few photographs of Dancing Deer's family on the stand.

"Seems like years," she said.

"It was only weeks," Brave Eagle said. They kissed and the touch of her skin, the scent of her body, excited him and as they stood in the bedroom doorway.

Touching her again brought a rush of desire to Brave Eagle and Onashola responded. She walked backwards to the bed, and lay down and his kisses rained upon her neck.

They were hungry for each other, and the stress of the weeks of the quest for their daughters heightened their desire. After their passionate reunion, they lay back and talked.

"You are going with me this time," Brave Eagle said.

"What about Betty? She's alone." Onashola snuggled into Brave Eagle, her head upon his chest, twirling her fingers through his hair. He wrapped his arm around her.

"She won't come with us. "

"We have to end this, Brave Eagle."

"What you mean is...we end McEver if we are ever to live in peace."

"Exactly what I mean."

"We'll see. He is soon to find his mining company expelled from the Black Hills. "

"He will fight back. "

"So will we. Do we leave South Dakota?"

"It's not like you to run away from a fight," Onashola observed. "Would you not miss this land?"

"This land was ruined the day Custer set foot upon it."

"It was more than Custer."

"Custer," Brave Eagle reminisced, " They made him into a hero in all the books, disregarding the fact he got all his men killed. The last stand, they call it." Brave Eagle raised his eyebrows, "Now it is McEver's turn to play last stand."

The next morning, Brave Eagle and Onashola returned to Rapid City, escorted by four Sioux braves. The plan was to pack for a trip to Denver, and leave the braves to protect Mrs. Pettigrew. Their trip was about to be delayed.

Maka and Wishiwu bought groceries and settled into the Denver home, awaiting Bobby's grandparents. They called Bobby, "Little brother."

"When Momma and Poppa come, I want to live here. Maybe we can talk them into staying," Maka said.

"Who owns this house now that Bobby's parents are dead?" Wishiwu asked.

"Bobby, I suppose."

Every day, they brought Bobby to Larry's house to play. Larry's mother asked about any developments with the grandparents.

"Any word yet?"

"No. We have mail, but not from them."

"Your parents?"

"Not yet. I wondered, though, does Bobby get to keep the house?"

"Oh, there is a mortgage, I am sure," Mary said. "When the grandparents arrive, they will sort through bills, and all sorts of legal arrangements. You can't live there. Sooner or later the bank will show up wanting to get paid."

"We could buy the house. We have some money," Maka said.

"How old are you again?"

Maka thought a second because she could not remember what she told the woman. "Eighteen."

"You're not, are you? You better wait for your parents to get her."

The same day, two letters arrived. They recognized their father's handwriting on a letter posted from Rapid City.

"Dear Maka and Wishiwu,

I am happy you are safe. I went to San Francisco, but you left. Your mother and I will come for you. Please stay where you are. With love, Father."

Wishiwu read over Maka's shoulder. "They are coming to get us!"

The second letter came from Bobby's grandparents.

"Dear Maka,

Thank you so much for caring and looking out for Bobby. We are very saddened by the death of our daughter and her husband. It is so tragic Bobby is alone in this world, but lucky he found such remarkable young women to help him. We cannot come to Denver to get him. My husband is in a wheelchair, and I can't leave him. Bobby's father has a sister in Denver but cannot find her address anywhere. We think best that Bobby live with her. Her name is Gladys, and she can take guardianship. If she can't, we will get him to Iowa. We can't properly care for a six-year old boy, though we would try to find a home for him. We don't want him to end out in an orphanage. That's a last resort. So, please find his Denver aunt and write us back. If you can't find her, we will have to get him here." Sincerely, Madeleine Bailey, Ames, Iowa.

"We're not taking him to that wretched aunt," Maka said to her sister.

"What's it say?" Bobby asked, tugging at Maka's sleeve.

"Your grandparents can't come here. They want us to take you."

"I want to stay here with you."

"Yeah," Wishiwu agreed. "When momma and poppa get here, let's buy this house and live in Denver."

" I do know one thing," Maka said.

"What?"

"Bobby's not going to that aunt's to live."

"I hate her," Bobby said. "I'll run away."

The next morning, there was an urgent knock on the door of the Elmwood house. Wishiwu opened it; two blue-coated policemen pushed her aside.

"Where's the boy?"

Maka stepped into the room, saw the police and ran for Bobby's room. The police gave chase and as Maka attempted to pick Bobby up from his bed where he slept, they brusquely shoved her.

"Step aside, Miss. Don't interfere. We're taking the boy."

"Where?"

"To his relatives."

Bobby stirred and opened his eyes to find himself in the arms of a burly, mustachioed policeman. He did a double take and realized they were taking him away from Maka.

"No! I want to stay with Maka and Wishiwu!"

"Come along."

The policemen carried Bobby out of the house and Maka and Wishiwu watched helplessly from the front porch. Bobby's aunt and uncle waited in a carriage, and the policeman put Bobby inside. As the carriage pulled away, Bobby stared back from a window in the carriage and he waved at them.

"Now what?" Wishiwu asked, sitting on the steps of the porch.

"We have their address. We'll get him back."

"They'll only take him back again and we'll get in trouble with the police."

"I'm surprised they didn't take us to the juvenile hall. That's coming next. We can't leave. Momma and Poppa will come here."

"What if they didn't get our letter?'

"We better send another one. "

As they stepped back inside the house, another car came down the street.

"Get inside."

The car parked in front of the house, and the same two policemen bolted from the car.

"Grab the money. Let's get out of here!"

Wishiwu retrieved the satchel with the money and they ran for the back door as the policemen knocked at the door. They ran from the back door into a small back yard, opened the gate to the alley and ran.

"Larry's house!"

They opened the alley gate to Larry's house and knocked on the back door.

Mary, Larry's mother, peeked out the window to see who was there first, then opened the door.

"Please hide us! The police are looking for us!" Maka shouted.

"What did you do?"

"Nothing. I think Bobby's aunt must have complained."

"I'll take you into the cellar."

She led them into a musty, damp cellar that contained a workbench, some infant's toys and a bunch of boxes.

"Stay here. I'll tell you when the policemen leave."

"What's going on, mother?" Larry asked from atop the stairs.

"Go to your room, Larry!"

Mary took a cup of coffee with her, and sat down on her own front porch, where she saw the police car parked in the street three doors away. The policemen came out of the house, and noticed her sitting out on the porch and walked over to her.

"Have you seen the two girls that live in this house?" one of them asked.

"I met them."

"Did you see where they went?"

"No. I came outside. I haven't seen them. What do you want them for?"

"They can't live in the house, we need to talk to them."

"They didn't do anything wrong?"

"No. The aunt and uncle are taking the house, as we understand."

"They are moving in?"

"I don't know. If you see the young girls, have them come down to the police station."

"I will."

The policemen left, and Mary returned to the cellar.

"Well, you can't stay in the house any longer. They want you to report to the police station."

"That we're not going to do," Maka pronounced.

"Bobby's aunt and uncle are taking the house. Maybe they'll be moving in," Mary said.

"Bobby hates his aunt!" Wishiwu said.

"Let's go back and get our clothes," Maka said. "We'll find another place to live and send Momma and Poppa the new address."

"What about Bobby? We can't leave him with his aunt!" Wishiwu protested.

"When Momma and poppa come, we'll take him to Iowa."

"You can't take the boy," Mary cautioned. "The court will decide who gets guardianship, the grandparents or the aunt."

"Maka, remember, the grandparents wrote to let him stay with the aunt."

Maka pursed her lips. "He's best off with us!"

Mary did a double take. "If you take Bobby, you would be in serious trouble."

"That's us, huh, Wishiwu? Outlaws!" she put her arm around her sister's shoulders and they both managed to laugh for the first time since the kidnappers took them from Rapid City.

"If you don't mind sleeping on the floor, you can stay in our house until your parents arrive," Mary offered. We have extra blankets, a floor, but otherwise, where you'd stay. There are no hotels close by."

Maka and Wishiwu nodded back.

Two days past. Three. Four. Two more letters were sent to Rapid City, without a word in reply.

CHAPTER 11

⚜

BRAVE EAGLE AND Onashola led four braves into Rapid City: Running Moose, Standing Tree, Thomas Stone, and Slow Water, assembled with the help of Dancing Deer and Black Elk. They were younger braves from families that settled on the reservation. Now in their twenties, they had never experienced war first hand, still they were well trained in archery and the use of knives and after learning of the evil McEver, welcomed a chance to right some wrongs.

Running Moose, Standing Tree and Slow Water were Cheyenne. Running Moose earned his name by outrunning a bull moose after he interrupted a moose that was in the act of stomping a wild dog. Standing Tree, his brother, was with him at the time and managed to climb a tree and watched his friend outrun the moose, before he also swung himself into a tree. The moose tried to push the tree down before giving up.

Onashola was a legend at the reservation, remembered as the one who carried her dead child in the papoose. In some small way, revenge upon McEver was revenge for Wounded Knee. Brave Eagle warned them of a potential battle with cowboys and they enthusiastically enlisted, persuading their friends Slow Water and Thomas Stone to join.

Slow Water was a giant of a boy, 18 years old, 6 feet 7 and all muscle. For a solid year, he had the assignment of breaking stones to be used for housing and doing that job had built rippling muscles. He was undefeated in the bare fisted boxing matches. The tribe believed he would have bested John L. Sullivan, but Sullivan had retired and was no longer in his prime. Still, he had a future in boxing.

Thomas Stone was the opposite, a short boy, 5 feet 5, only one hundred and twenty pounds. His parents had converted to Catholicism and he was a firm Christian with a strong sense of justice. He was 17, the best friend of Slow Water, and intended to attend college and practice law. He helped Slow Water at his boxing matches, toweling him off and giving him water between rounds.

Two horse carriages carried supplies, one driven by Brave Eagle and Onashola, the other by Standing Tree and the rest rode on horses. They passed through Rapid City at sunset, a bright orange glow filtering through cirrus clouds. As they approached his house, Brave Eagle raised his hand to halt. An automobile and two horses were parked in front of the house.

He directed Slow Water to hold the horses, while he pulled bows and arrows from the carriage.

"No guns, let's be quiet."

Brave Eagle and Onashola stealthily approached their house with Running Moose, Slow Water and Standing Tree. A cowboy sat in front of Betty at the kitchen table, facing the window, with two cowboys behind her. McEver's assistant, Jenkins, sat across from Betty, his back to the window. Brave Eagle leaned in, and could not hear what they said, but Betty kept shaking her head.

"You, go around to the front door. The men have guns. Bows ready when you come in. Thomas come over here and tell us and we will go in. Take the man at the table. If he goes for a gun, shoot."

Brave Eagle and Onashola crouched at the front door, their bows strung.

"It's going to make the creaking sound," Onashola reminded Brave Eagle. "All these years, I told you to fix it!"

Brave Eagle smiled at the reminder.

Brave Eagle and Onashola took two arrows, but both had knives on their waists. Brave Eagle took a deep breath and put his hand on the doorknob, and gave the signal. He twisted the handle and he and Onashola opened the door.

The creak of the door alerted the two cowboys, as Brave Eagle and Onashola entered with drawn bows. The men reached for their holstered pistols, and as they pulled them from their holsters, Brave Eagle and Onashola shot. Both arrows lodged deep into each cowboy's shoulders and they plummeted to the floor in agony. The three braves burst in from the front door, and Jenkins raised his hands in surrender.

"No! No! Don't shoot!"

"Kill him?" Standing Tree asked from across the room.

"No, we will let him bring a message to McEver."

Betty put her face in her hands and cried and Onashola comforted her.

"What are these?" Brave Eagle asked the assistant. Several documents lay on the table.

"McEver wanted this! I just work for him!"

"What?"

"He wanted her to sign this deed. "

Brave Eagle glanced over the deed then his attention turned to another document.

"Last will and testament. I, Betty Pettigrew, being of sound mind.... What is this?"

"McEver wanted her property when she died."

"I suppose he wanted her to die soon."

Onashola stayed behind with Betty, and Brave Eagle led Jenkins to the carriage. The wounded cowboys were dragged out of the house and dumped into the carriage.

It was a mile or so to the ranch. Brave Eagle pulled on a canvas jacket. It was one of those nights in South Dakota where the stars shone bright and as he rode down the dark road, he gazed at the constellations and found the one with the man shooting a bow. Orion, the hunter. That is me, tonight, he thought. Who were those cowboys? They can't be good men, or they would not threaten an old lady out of her possessions, working for McEver. Their mothers must not love them. Why else would you wander out to this place for such an occupation? What price did the evil pay? Take McEver, a lifetime of riches from ill-gotten gains, and his payback does not come until he is old. Onashola told Brave Eagle how McEver treated his young wife. She was a prostitute, but might find redemption. He told the other braves not to harm her.

Where could Brave Eagle, Onashola and their daughters find a place of peace and tranquility? He expected he would live out his days, never finding that special place, not until he died, whether it was God or Jesus, or even Crazy Horse waiting for him. He envisioned Custer, sitting on a throne next to Jesus.

"Now, I even the score," Custer would say.

He shook the death thoughts from his head. It was not a good idea to welcome Heaven into your mind when you face an enemy, lest you seek death.

They arrived at the ranch, and stopped about one hundred yards from the front door.

"How many men work for McEver?"

"Five more, not counting me," Jenkins said.

"Where are the five cowboys?"

"They will be in the back house, over there. It will be McEver and his wife in the ranch house. I don't want any part of this. I only work for him."

"You are part of this. Very much so. They took my wife, my daughters, tried to kill Mrs. Pettigrew."

"I'll help you if you spare me."

"Go tell McEver to prepare to die, because we are coming for him, and the braves here, they have not taken a scalp in many moons. Feel your own scalp, because within the hour, it will be gone from your head."

Standing Tree and Thomas Stone yanked both arrows out and the men both passed out. They dragged the wounded cowboys to the front of the house and placed them in sitting positions, propped up and tied to the horse trough. Standing Tree placed their arms around each other's shoulders, and they appeared to be two drinking buddies.

Jenkins knocked on the door, as Brave Eagle whistled and Standing Tree moved to the rear of the house.

"Thomas, you stay here and cover the house. The rest of you come with me. Tie the horses."

"Guns or bows?'

"Bring both. "

Brave Eagle and the other braves walked quietly to the dormitory of cowboys. They each carried a pistol, a knife in their belts, strung bows and a sheath on their shoulders.

They surrounded the house. Brave Eagle and Running Moose took a position at the front and the other braves at the rear. As the men positioned themselves, one of the cowboys came out the back door, and an arrow flew into his chest. The force of the strike caused him to fall back into the house, and the braves yelled a war cry and rushed the house.

Brave Eagle and Running Moose opened the front door, where the cowboys scrambled for their guns. Brave Eagle and Running Moose's arrows slammed into the backs of two of the men. One of them, crawling to his bunk, managed to reach his gun, shoot and wound Running Moose, but before he could get the second shot off, Running Moose slit his throat. The last man managed to run out the back door in the chaos and Slow Water gave chase. About two minutes later, a victory cry rang though the night.

Running Moose was shot in the thigh, and winced in pain and tore through his trousers with a knife to dislodge the bullet. "Hold on." Thomas said, so he administered to the brave's wounds. Brave Eagle ran outside and found Standing Tree holding a pistol aimed at McEver, who emerged from the house holding his wife as a human shield.

Standing tree hesitated at the sight of the woman, long enough for McEver to shoot at him. As Standing Tree fell wounded to the ground, McEver aimed to shot again, but Brave Eagle leapt from behind, and wrestled him to the ground. McEver's wife fell to her knees as Brave Eagle sat atop McEver, a knife at his throat.

"Piece of shit pile! You coward!" Josephine shrieked at McEver.

"Where's the other man?" Brave Eagle asked.

"Inside."

Brave Eagle motioned to the other men. "One more in the house. Try to take him alive, if you can. They have a different path to take."

"I hope they take your scalp, you shit!' the blonde woman yelled at McEver, who was pinned beneath Brave Eagle. She leaned over and spit on him.

"Go back into the house and be quiet!" Brave Eagle told her.

"I will pay you. How much do you want?' McEver pleaded.

Brave Eagle clamped his palm over McEver's mouth and pushed hard. "Don't talk of anything " He saw a man with no soul, a vacuum of a person. He may have been ten years older than Brave Eagle, but his face showed decay, crevices of guilt dug into his forehead. Brave Eagle smelled urine. The man pissed his pants. Feeling the dampness on his leg, he pulled McEver into a standing position.

The other braves brought Jenkins out of the house. "Don't kill me. I had nothing to do with any of this!"

"Yes he did!" the blonde shouted. "Cut off his balls and shove them down his throat! If you don't, I will!"

"Get inside!" Brave Eagle demanded.

Slow Water tied McEver's and Jenkins's hands and feet and pushed them into the back of the carriage and the entourage returned to Brave Eagle's house. They parked the carriage containing McEver in the barn overnight, and the next morning set out north to the Black Hills, with Onashola staying behind with Betty Pettigrew.

Sheriff Jameson was with Betty when Onashola returned.

"I just left. I just left. I'm sorry I didn't stay," Jameson apologized.

"Who knew they would come?" Betty shrugged. "What did you do?"

"There was a fight at the ranch. All McEver's men."

"Are they all dead?"

"Some are. The blonde woman must be here in Rapid City this morning. And McEver and his assistant, Brave Eagle are taking them to the Black Hills."

"What for?"

"Maybe to show him the hills."

"Did any of your braves get hurt?"

"Yes, but not bad. They are with Brave Eagle."

"Wish I could have helped. I don't know what life will be like in Rapid City without McEver and his cowboys. Might be peaceful. That will make my job easier."

If Rapid City did find peace, Jameson thought he could probably stay on the job a few more years. He was growing weary of it all, the drunks, and the shootings. Lately he'd required a two-hour nap every afternoon, letting his deputy take a shift on duty. What was he? Sixty-four years of age now. Many a time he'd heard of a sheriff his age getting gunned down right before he was about to hang up his pistol. He didn't want that fate. He desired his later years to be sitting out on a rocker somewhere beautiful and warm.

Brave Eagle had a destination in mind, a place he visited before. He had taken Onashola into the wooded hills when pregnant and they slept under the stars for three days, with Bone at their side, to talk about the future of their unborn baby and what they hoped and dreamed would come true for the baby that would become Maka. They took a journey when pregnant the second time, with Maka a year and a half old, to speculate on the dreams for their second baby and returned as a family on multiple occasions. Brave Eagle had located a secluded spot, where they slept in a shallow cave that protected them from the Dakota summer rains. Maka was a child who loved to talk, but Brave Eagle taught her the value of remaining still and quiet and pay attention to the rain, as they sat in the comfort of the cave.

"Where are you taking them?" Onashola asked as he left.

"The Black Hills."

"Oh. Don't tell me any more," she said.

It was about fifty miles from Rapid City to the Black Hills. They reached an overlook and Brave Eagle pointed to a rocky hill a half-mile away.

"There!"

He steered the horses along a ridge top, sitting on the carriage, while McEver and Jenkins lay flat inside the carriage. The braves followed behind the carriage, until Brave Eagle stopped, got off the carriage and looked at a hill that sloped downwards about 2000 feet.

Brave Eagle unhitched the horses from the carriage.

"Put the two of them sitting on the carriage," Brave Eagle instructed. Standing Tree and Thomas grabbed McEver and Jenkins and placed them on the front bench, and turned the carriage to face down the hill. Their hands and feet were still tied, and they stared to a valley far below.

McEver glanced down. "I will make you all rich men. You can have my hotels and my ranch."

Jenkins began to cry.

"Here, McEver, I have something to give you," Brave Eagle said. He withdrew a piece of paper from inside his shirt. "Here is the deed." He wadded the map and placed it inside McEver's shirt.

Brave Eagle moved to the back of the carriage with his men and ordered, "Push!"

They shoved the wagon, and it took off. The wagon careened down the hill and after traveling for thirty yards, hit a rock and flipped over, vaulting McEver and his aide high into the air. They screamed, terrified.

"Let's go," Brave Eagle said.

"Deer path," Standing Tree said, and they found easier footing descending in a narrow trail.

The carriage smashed to pieces. Two wheels remained attached to the carriage. Brave Eagle found Jenkins first. He put his fingertips to the man's neck, finding a pulse.

"This one lives."

"This one doesn't," Standing Tree observed, twenty feet further down the hill. McEver's head was at an odd angle, and his tied hands distorted behind his back.

"To the buzzards," Brave Eagle said, looking to the sky for the hungry birds. "The other one is meant to live if he survived."

They dragged Jenkins up the hill.

"We could wait for him to wake up and let him ride the horse," Thomas Stone suggested.

"I had to go to San Francisco in search of my daughters because of these men," Brave Eagle announced. "Let him have his own journey."

He untied the unconscious man's hands and feet. "Leave him. When he wakes up, he can walk."

"Cat prints," Slow Water observed, pointing to mountain lion paw prints on the ground. "If he does not wake up soon, he is meat."

Brave Eagle shrugged.

Brave Eagle felt this primeval urge, and raised and shouted a howl to the heavens, and so, too did his fellow braves join in. They joined arms in a circle and looked up into the sky and howled in unison.

He would kill any man who intended harm to his wife or daughters. In battles past, he took part in mutilating the dead, but he no longer had that inclination.

The next stage of the mission was to Denver, Colorado. This time he would take Onashola. He did not ever want to be separated again.

The group returned to Rapid City, and Brave Eagle realized they had some clean up work to do at the McEver ranch. They arrived at the ranch and dug a pit behind the barn, untied the two wounded cowboys from the horse trough and told them to be on their way.

Mrs. McEver loaded luggage to a horse cart when Brave Eagle and Standing Tree approached. She lifted a rifle into her shoulder and cocked.

"I know how to use it," she said.

Brave Eagle raised his hands. "We are not going to harm you. We are burying the cowboys."

"Since when do Indians bury the dead?"

"Since now. Where are you going?"

"What do you care? I'm not going to tell the sheriff. I'm leaving. Tennessee. This was a horrible experience. Did you kill them?"

"Your husband's not coming back."

She glanced back at the barn. "I wish I could drive that automobile, I wouldn't take a stagecoach."

"You're better off with company."

"I'm catching the coach in Rapid City. I'll have company before long. I always do. Men like me."

"You paid a pretty high price, marrying McEver."

"Tell you what, Mister Indian, sir. I'm leaving this house with enough money to last my lifetime, and all I had to do was sleep with this foul, toothless man for two years. From now on, I can pick who I want to sleep with and money ain't the issue."

"I wish you well. So, no word about what happened here?"

"Don't worry. What is it? You afraid of going to prison? For killing this thieving, terrible man? They ought to give you a medal. Don't bother locking the door. Take what you want. Those fellas out at the barn can make it their house for all I care."

Mrs. McEver climbed into the carriage and shook the reins.

"Giddy up! Goodbye, Mr. Indian! You'll never see me in these parts again."

The team completed the job of dumping the corpses into the pit, covering them up. Brave Eagle thanked them for their help and promised a return visit to Pine Ridge, once they had their daughters back in hand. The men stayed the night in the cowboy's dormitory, which they found stocked with food and drink.

Brave Eagle rode the horse cart back home. It was early evening and in the twilight, the house lights on, and Onashola standing on the porch. She took off running to meet him.

Brave Eagle smiled at the sight of his wife, running in his direction. How many women so effortlessly glide down the road like she did, at such a speed? Beat me up, rob me, test me with every possible obstacle, oh man in the sky, but still, you gave me Onashola and Maka and Wishiwu, and I am grateful!

She climbed into the seat next to him and showered him with kisses.

"Where are the others?"

"Staying the night at McEver's."

"What?"

"He is not going to bother us any more."

"His wife rode passed here not an hour ago. What happened?'

"He's gone. All his cowboys are gone, too. It's over. The braves returned to the reservation. We need to make our way to Denver in the morning."

They rode the carriage back to the house. Betty came out to the porch to greet them.

"And?"

Brave Eagle dusted his denim jeans off as he dismounted the carriage with Onashola.

"Let's say McEver and his cowboys are not going to bother you any more."

"What happened to him?"

"He's at the bottom of the Black Hills."

"The ranch hands?'

"Gone."

"And your braves?"

"Pine Ridge."

"Well, I have some good news for you, too. Come inside."

They sat at the kitchen table, the same one where Brave Eagle and Onashola put arrows into the chests of the cowboys.

"Now we bring them back." Brave Eagle held Onashola's hand across the table.

Maka and Wishiwu were well cared for by Mary Gray, her husband, Brett, and little Larry. Mary was four months pregnant with her second child.

At night, after Larry went to bed, Mary had long conversations with Maka and Wishiwu. Mary had finished high school and attended a secretarial college for a year. She worked in a department store as a secretary, and her husband Brett was the store manager. Brett finished college at the University of Colorado in Denver. When Larry was born, Mary stayed home. They lived modestly, and on a bookshelf had nine books including

Pride and Prejudice, which Maka started to read. Wishiwu read another book, Silas Marner.

Every day, they walked over to Bobby's house to check the mail and finally there was a letter addressed to them.

May 8,
Dear Maka and Wishiwu,
We are leaving now for Denver and are so glad to know where you are. Father followed you to San Francisco and he managed to find the baseball team. God blessed you survived.
Please stay where you are and we are on the way. We love and cherish you, since the day you born.
Love,
Onashola

It was springtime in Denver, and the creeks gushed with snowmelt. The weather was dry, with chilly nights and pleasant days. Maka and Wishiwu took daily walks to Cherry Creek Park with Mary and Larry. One Saturday, the family took a picnic to the park, where a track meet took place and men competed in a number of races: the hurdles, the sprints and distance runs, the javelin and the shot put.

They were particularly interested in the mile run, four times around a circular track.

"How long will it take them?" Maka asked.

"I should expect under five minutes. Not long," Brett said.

Eight men lined up and Brett checked his watch. They sat on the grass, near the first curve of the oval track. The men wore singlets and short pants. A man signaled for the start and the racers passed by their picnic. The men packed together as they turned, at a strong pace. When they reached the end of the first lap, Brett announced, "Seventy two seconds!"

The runners reached the second lap in two minutes twenty three seconds. Midway through the third lap, the group began to spread out and three men emerged from the group. The third lap was reached in three minutes and thirty-seven seconds. A bell clanged signaling the final lap, and two men pulled fifteen yards from the third man, and headed down the straight away with a lunge at the finish line. Both men fell.

"Four minutes and forty seven seconds! Not bad in this thin air!" Brett observed.

Maka glanced at Wishiwu. "Are you thinking what I'm thinking?"

"Yes. I bet we beat that."

"Let's try when everyone is gone."

"Think you can run faster?" Brett asked. "I doubt it!"

"We don't have the right shoes, so we'll try barefoot." They took off their petticoats from beneath their dresses, and would run in the skirts and white blouses Mary gave them.

An hour later, after the crowd dispersed, Maka and Wishiwu toed the starting line and Brett shouted, "Go!"

The girls took off in a hurry, with Maka taking the lead. They came to the end of the first lap and Brett looked at his watch, "Seventy four seconds!"

In the second lap, they both gave out. "I can't keep up," Wishiwu said, and dropped back away from her sister. They continued to slow, and when they reached the end of the second lap, Maka stopped, bent over and gasped for breath. Wishiwu came a few seconds later, her face red, and fell to her knees.

"Two minutes and forty five seconds! Barefoot, in dresses. Amazing."

"You girls are tremendous," Mary Gray said, putting her arms around Maka, who still struggled to breathe. Maka recovered and caught her breath, she said, "I thought we could beat those men."

"So did I. We ran our mile in South Dakota under six minutes. I f we tried, we could get under five," Wishiwu added.

"The air is too thin," Maka said. "Those men wore hardly any clothes. They had an advantage."

"You can't expect to go out without any training," Brett commented. "Those men practice a lot to run those times. They are trying for the Olympic team in 1908."

"They don't let girls in the Olympics, do they?" Maka asked.

"Afraid not."

"Well, they should!"

CHAPTER 12

❧

THE GRAY FAMILY returned from their Saturday picnic and noticed a carriage parked in front of Bobby's house. His aunt and uncle emerged from the house and took two large sacks from the carriage, paid the driver and the horses trotted off. Bobby sat on the front porch steps as Maka and Wishiwu approached.

He waved and his Aunt Gladys grabbed him by the collar.

"You're not going anywhere!"

The Grays walked over to meet the new neighbors.

"Are you moving in?" Brett asked.

"Yes we are," Gladys replied sharply.

"I'm Brett Gray. I believe you've met my wife, Mary. Our son Larry and Bobby's cousins, Maka and Wishiwu."

"I know who you are." Gladys' husband Rolly came out of the house, his face red and sweaty. "I'm Bobby's aunt Gladys."

"Rolly," the large uncle extended a sweaty hand to Brett.

"Glad Bobby is back in the neighborhood," Mary said.

"Can I play with Larry?" Bobby asked.

"We have to unpack," Gladys scolded. "There's work to do here, if you will excuse us."

"Yes, see you soon," Brett said.

As they walked away from the house, Brett whispered to his wife, "What a crabby lady!"

In the early evening, Maka and Wishiwu positioned themselves outside the dining room window.

Aunt Gladys and Rolly ate at the dinner table. Bobby sat in a chair, drinking a glass of milk.

"Now, we have a house, at least. You better find a job soon. How much money is left?" Gladys asked.

"Six hundred dollars."

"You had to go and lose your job."

"Well, at least we won't pay rent any more."

"How much do you think we could sell this house for?"

"I never sold a house. A couple thousand dollars."

"We can't afford him," she said, glancing at Bobby. "The grandparents can bail us out with some money."

"Maybe."

"Well, something has to give soon. You either find a job within a couple of months or the house will be sold. "

Maka motioned to Wishiwu and they walked back to Larry's house.

"So, they need money."

The first two days after Bobby and his aunt and uncle moved back, Maka and Wishiwu knocked on the door and asked the Aunt if Bobby could play. Both times they were refused.

"No. He has chores to do," was the explanation.

A few days later, at eight o'clock in the morning, Maka and Wishiwu sat on the front porch with Larry and Mary. They watched children walk down the sidewalk to their nearby elementary school. A carriage pulled up in front of Bobby's house, and a man and a woman emerged. The man wore a black suit and the woman a white cotton dress covered by a shawl.

"Momma! Poppa!"

Brave Eagle dropped the suitcase and Onashola did not wait for the bag the man extended from the carriage. They met their children, smothering them with hugs, kisses, crying with joy.

"Do we have stories to tell!" Maka said.

"We do, too," Onashola cried, wiping away her tears. "Shall we go inside the house?"

"We are staying there," Maka pointed to Larry's house, where Larry and his mother stood watching. "Bobby's aunt and uncle are here now."

They carried their suitcases to Larry's house, where they met Larry and Mary. When Brave Eagle and Onashola were alone with their daughters, Brave Eagle asked, "Somewhere we can talk?"

"Let's go to the park," Maka said. "Cherry Creek is right down the street."

Brave Eagle took off his suit jacket, sweating in the dry heat.

They reached the park and found an empty bench. Brave Eagle sat with Onashola, while Maka and Onashola sat on the ground next to the bench. It was a weekday morning, and the park was mostly populated with older people walking around the dirt road.

"Tell us."

"You tell them," Wishiwu said.

Maka sighed. "Well, the men took us away and we cut through the ties and when they stopped in Pierre, we ran out and tried to get away but they caught us. We rode the train to San Francisco with them and as soon as we stopped we got away."

"And took some of their money with us," Wishiwu added.

"We were afraid to go to the train station at first and run into them so we decided to stay in San Francisco for a couple days, and the earthquake hit. We found Bobby. His parents died, so we decided to return him here and stay until we connected with you."

Wishiwu covered her face and cried, and Onashola sat down on the ground with her, holding her.

"Do we go back to South Dakota?' Wishiwu asked. "We don't want to live there any more."

"It's safe now."

"When are we going back?"

"Tomorrow."

"Something else, Poppa. This boy we found in San Francisco, Bobby. We want to bring him to his grandparents in Iowa. He's living with his mean aunt and uncle, and they don't want him. They want money. We should take Bobby back to his grandparents. He told us the aunt hits him."

"We can talk about that later."

They told their parents about the earthquake in San Francisco, and learned what their parents went through - their father's trip to San Francisco, their mother's capture and escape.

"We lived a lifetime in two months," Maka sighed.

"Maka looks like a grown woman now."

"What about me? Wishiwu asked.

"Girls should not go through what you did. But we are all together now."

"Except Bone died."

"Oh!"

They stayed in the park the better part of the afternoon, talking. By the time they returned to Larry's house, children returned from school. Brave Eagle asked Maka to take a thousand dollars from their satchel and he escorted his oldest daughter over to Bobby's house.

One hour later, they returned, with Maka holding Bobby by the hand.

"We're going to Iowa," Brave Eagle told Onashola. "A brief detour, wherever Ames, Iowa is. ""Oh, Bobby!" Wishiwu hugged the little blond haired boy.

Brave Eagle nodded his approval.

Brave Eagle and Onashola agreed for Bobby to live with them. He was such a loving and smart little boy. They were amazed a boy who had not even started school read, multiplied and divided, and on the trip, revealed a sweet singing voice.

He had a lightning quick little mind. Once, Maka asked him to multiply seven times nine divided by three and Bobby asked where she put the parenthesis.

Ames was a small college town, the home of Iowa State University and his grandfather was a retired professor of literature.

They met the grandparents at their home two blocks from campus. Bobby's grandfather sat in a wheel chair on the porch. His wife stood behind the chair as the Heard family mounted the steps, with Wishiwu holding Bobby's hand.

"Grandma! Grandpa!" Little Bobby embraced his silver-haired grandparents. Grandpa Bailey had a sparkly face, with a strong upper body and skinny, withered legs. Grandma Bailey was a thin, fragile woman, stricken with arthritis. She wore gloves that protected aching hands. Despite the pain in her hands and joints, she managed a warm smile.

In the course of the day, Brave Eagle and Onashola both learned of how the Baileys met on the first day Grandpa taught at Iowa State, when a young sophomore girl asked him a question in class that impressed him with its insightfulness.

"I'm not from Iowa, no," Grandpa told Brave Eagle as they conversed on the porch.

Brave Eagle sat on a rocking chair, drinking tea.

"I'm from Hartford, Connecticut, a town that appreciated literature and I took to the classics. I went to Yale, my life got interrupted a bit in the War Between the States."

"Is that when you got injured?"

"No. I fell off a horse here, about twenty years ago. I came here out of Columbia in New York. First and only college teaching job."

"What did you teach?"

"Homer. The Iliad and the Odyssey. My whole life is Achilles, Helen, and Ulysses."

"I should read those books. I never got around to," Brave Eagle admitted.

"Where it all starts."

"I bet I read half the books in the Rapid City library."

"Oh, my grandson, his mother and father started with him."

"Sorry about them, sir."

"Yes. To die because they wanted to hear an opera singer. I suppose everyone goes to a certain place when God believes the time. I never thought I would outlive my only child. It was bad enough when they moved to Colorado but this, this...." He choked back his emotions and did not talk for a few minutes and Brave Eagle did not intrude on the silence.

"I thought she would be a professor, too, growing up, so bright."

"Bobby inherited her intelligence."

"Yes, yes. How are we are going to handle raising him. It will be hard."

"My wife and I, and our daughters, would like to raise Bobby. We live in South Dakota, and we promise we would bring him back frequently for visits. "

"Why don't you stay here a while? We'll talk. Do you mind sleeping on a sofa?"

"Onashola and I used to sleep on the ground. Of course not."

Grandpa and Grandma Bailey agreed to send Bobby, but with one stipulation. They saved money for Bobby's college, and Brave Eagle and Onashola promised he would be educated.

They stayed in Ames for four days before packing up and saying goodbye. The Baileys were transfixed by the stories of Brave Eagle and Onashola's adventures.

"We've led a sedate life, my lord," Grandma laughed. "We live in this little college town peaceful and quiet and you're in the Wild West. "

"Grandpa commented. "Brave Eagle and Onashola lived their own Odyssey."

"I think, from now on, we will seek quiet," Brave Eagle said, with Onashola nodding her assent. "We've had enough excitement for five lifetimes. Let's hope Bobby has a more tranquil upbringing."

Maka and Wishiwu never knew grandparents. Grandma Bailey seemed to live in the kitchen and loved to knit and read. Grandpa Bailey gave Brave Eagle two dog-eared copies of the Iliad and Odyssey, full of notes written in the margins.

They made their way from Iowa to Omaha, on to Sioux Falls, and finally Rapid City, by train and stagecoach. They arrived at the front door of their home and were confronted with a crew of men removing debris from Betty's house and placing the charred wood in carts.

Betty had made cherry pies and cookies.

"I'm going to rebuild the house," Betty told them. "My, going to be tight around here. I can stay at the hotel."

"No, we have room," Brave Eagle smiled.

"He's right. We are so happy to be all together again, we sleep on the earth, and the way we used to."

"Bobby is adorable," Betty added. "He found the perfect home."

Brave Eagle and Onashola sat on the front porch as, in the front yard, Maka instructed Bobby on how to swing a bat, as Wishiwu tossed a base-ball underhanded for him to hit. Each time Bobby swung, he closed his eyes and missed.

"Bobby, watch for the ball. You can't hit if you can't see it," Maka told him.

Bobby put his hands in the dirt and rubbed them together, held the bat back the way Maka showed him and Wishiwu tossed. The bat smacked the ball in a line drive.

"Yay! I hit it!"

"You run around the bases."

"I want to hit again."

Brave Eagle pointed at a row of sparrows sitting on a tree branch in the front yard.

"They are watching. I wonder what they are thinking."

"Get out of the way!" Onashola laughed.

Brave Eagle put his arm around Onashola's shoulders and leaned over to smell her hair, and the skin on her neck. He inhaled and stroked her lustrous dark hair.

"I understand the expression, home sweet home."

Onashola smiled, put her head on his shoulder, and kissed him.

How many years left on this earth? He valued and cherished every waking moment with Onashola and his daughters, and now this little boy Bobby.

Would they stay in Rapid City much longer? Would one McEver go, only to be replaced by another? That seemed to be the way of life.

The ball rolled to the porch and Brave Eagle retrieved it. The red stitching from the ball was loose and the cowhide beginning to peel off the ball.

"You need a new ball soon."

He threw to Wishiwu, who caught it in her glove, and sat back on the porch.

"What day is today?'

"Wednesday."

"Will you go back to the library tomorrow?"

"Yes I will. I am sure Betty brought in some new books."

"So we return to our life."

"Yes. We do. Summer is almost here. Let's hope it is less eventful than this spring!"

Brave Eagle pulled off his boots and Onashola waved at her nose. "We all need baths! Those feet. Let me draw you a bath."

"In a while. I enjoy watching them play. Remember this day. If your life passes before your eyes when you die, this is what I want - you sitting with me on the porch, Maka and Wishiwu playing baseball in the yard."

A blanket on the porch, next to the rocking chair, lay where Bone sat regally. At times like this, Bone sauntered over to his side and positioned his head so Brave Eagle stroked him.

The day would come when Brave Eagle would join his dog, and many years later, Onashola, but at this moment, in this lifetime, every strand of his wife's hair, every crack of a bat hitting a ball, every sparrow that sat upon a tree branch, and every smell of a cherry pie coming from the kitchen, told Brave Eagle life provided many blessings. It would never be a path without obstacles.

"Throw him a curve ball," Maka shouted.

Wishiwu wound up and pitched the ball to Bobby. He hit the ball cleanly, a grounder to Wishiwu left.

"Good hit! Bobby hit the curve!"

Brave Eagle took his dusty green socks off. Onashola was right. He needed a bath. So, he got up from the porch, gazed back at his daughters enjoying their baseball game, and gazed beyond, at the South Dakota hills. He had gone from nothing to something to nothing to something back again.

Jenkins, after recovering from his wounds, took a train to Sacramento, where Leo McEver's surviving older brother, Mark, still lived. Mark was 79 years old and retired to a hacienda in the foothills outside of the city. He was out of the mining business, and had divested his San Francisco hotels prior to the earthquake, but still owned a Sacramento farm.

His wife was a Mexican immigrant, Lucita, 39 years old, he found working in his fields when she was 19. He was married, but when his wife died the next year, he brought Lucita into his home. He had two sons from his first marriage and a son and a daughter with Lucita.

Mark McEver's two oldest sons were his business partners. The eldest, Ralph had unsuccessfully run for California senator two years prior. The second son, James, was a problem. James was 30, already having spent time in the California prison for fraud.

Jenkins sought an audience with Mark McEver on his ranch house, a mansion that made Leo McEver's property in South Dakota resemble a cabin.

"All right. From the beginning," Mark McEver sat in what resembled a throne: an oversized chair with an ottoman for him to rest his feet. Like his brother, he clutched a cane in one hand. Mark had long, shaggy white hair and spectacles. He was the same physical build as Leo, long and lanky and thin.

His son, James sat across the room, to the left of Jenkins who faced the throne, standing.

"Leo owned multiple businesses in Rapid City. A hotel, a bar, a cattle ranch, and a mine. In San Francisco, the two hotels were destroyed in the earthquake."

"Sit there!" Mark commanded, and Jenkins sat on a rocker on the right of the room. A buffalo head loomed on the wall behind Mark McEver and a painting of wood nymphs dancing hung on the wall behind James. Jenkins inhaled the odor of pies baking from a nearby kitchen.

"After five years, the mines came up empty, and the whole mining industry of South Dakota dried up. People moved away and the hotel closed, the bar sold. Your brother lived off his wealth from here."

"He had enough to last."

"No, he didn't. He went through most of it."

"How did he die?"

"That's what I am getting to. So a man in Rapid City struck gold, sold the gold and sealed his mine and kept secret. His mine was on land adjacent to Leo's. Leo tried to buy the land, but the man refused, and well, Leo got mad and had him killed. When things started getting tough, his men tried to find a map and they when to the man's widow and got a key from her safe led to a San Francisco safe deposit box. The men took two young girls who lived next door as hostages."

"Why?"

"Wasn't the plan. Leo sent men to intercept them and the girl's father beat them to San Francisco with a second key, then the earthquake, we came up empty and Leo took the girls' mother as a hostage, but she escaped, and the next thing, they invaded the ranch with a bunch of Indian warriors. They took us out to the Black Hills and pushed Leo and me down a mountain in a cart. Leo died and it took me months to get over all my broken bones."

"Leo was so stupid. What do you want me to do?"

"I thought you might still be interested in gold, somewhere in the hills. And you might want to take revenge for your brother."

"I'll do that," James nodded.

"You never liked Leo," Mark smirked.

"He was my uncle and they murdered him."

"After he took two girls and a woman hostage. Sounds like he played with fire."

"Oh, fire. I forgot, he burned the wife of the miner's house down, too."

"What's in all this for us, Jenkins."

"He has a nice ranch, unattended. And as his closest relative, it is yours, according to the will."

"Aha! Promising. Although I'll never move to South Dakota. And what else?"

"Potential for gold. But you must deal with Brave Eagle."

"Who?"

"The father of those girls. A half-breed Indian, the one who killed your brother."

"Why should we bother with him?'

"He's in the way, that's all. And..I would like revenge..."

"I will take care of it. Father, the ranch? You don't want it."

Mark shrugged. "Sure. Why not? Is it a working ranch?"

"Could be. It's big enough for an entire cattle operation. What I think should be done is go out find gold, take as much as possible, seal and claim it came from one of Leo's mines. They'll never know," Jenkins interjected.

"Why didn't Leo do that himself?"

"He tried. He never found it. It's a few thousand acres and covered up well."

"Isn't there something like a mining expert?"

"Not that I know of. If there was, he'd be the richest man in America."

"Tell you what. James, you're lying around Sacramento doing nothing. Rapid City is yours now. Make something out of it."

"I will. First thing I'll get rid of the Indian."

"Brave Eagle, Won't be easy. And his wife."

"Then what?"

"You need to not be connected."

"Easy. Some men here I can hire. I pay them and they do the job and leave."

"Whatever you want to do. The ranch is yours. As far as the mine, well, I wouldn't invest too much time," Mark McEver advised. "When do you want to go?"

"Soon as I can hire some men. How do you get to Rapid City?"

"A train rides to Des Moines, then a stage."

"Where do I buy horses?"

"Sioux City."

"All right. And what do you want out of this?"

"We can talk on the way, but Brave Eagle is a start."

As they departed his uncle's office, Jenkins said to James, "Brave Eagle rode with Crazy Horse."

"Crazy Horse? He's dead. And so is Brave Eagle!"

They arrived almost a year to the day after the San Francisco, Earthquake. Rapid City was abuzz with the arrival of the arrival of a caravan of carriages, two motorcars, a dozen horses and a dozen men. And they paraded past Brave Eagle and Onashola's home.

Brave Eagle, Onashola, Maka and Wishiwu sat on their porch. From the motorcar at the front of the procession, they caught their first glimpse of twenty-nine yard old James McEver, who peeked out from the back and glared at them.

"Here comes trouble," Brave Eagle commented.

"The nephew is what I heard," Onashola nodded.

"I don't even have to guess what they are up to. Pack mules!" He pointed to four mules, laden with picks and shovels on their backs.

Down the road a couple hundred yards, Sheriff Jameson also watched the procession from the porch of Betty Pettigrew's rebuilt home.

"Come out here, Betty!" he shouted to her. She came out to the porch wearing flour-spattered apron.

"More McEvers. Now what?"

"They intend to do some mining. All the other miners have gone on to other things. At least they'll have the hills to themselves."

"And undoubtedly, they will head straight for, well, it's not my property any more. But if they make a claim, odds are, it's on Sioux land now. "

"The North Homestake Company found a vein over in the Maitland area, so there's still some. But they have one hundred and twenty five miners. "

James McEver brought with him fourteen miners, four ranch hands, Jenkins, a geologist he hired fro the South Dakota School f Mines, Barrett, and two whores, Angel and Greta.

The miners and ranch hands housed together the first night in the dorm outside the ranch, but the miners set out for the hills the first morning. Brave Eagle followed at a comfortable distance.

Barrett, a professor at the university, a weather-beaten nervous man, who claimed to know everything about the mining of the hills, led the miners and their burros nineteen miles from Rapid City, into a ravine previously mined by Leo McEver's troop. A creek bisected the ravine and while he motioned the men to stay put, he ventured on foot down the creek a half-mile when he gave a shout and the men followed. They set up camp atop a hill above the creek. Brave Eagle noted their resting place and returned home.

The next day, Brave Eagle trekked into the hills and foraged the surrounding area for materials, carrying his bow and arrow, some cloth and a small container of kerosene. He found an antelope carcass and severed the head and legs and collected two six foot tree branches.

He waited after sunset for three hours and under a full moon, descended into the mining camp. The camp consisted of three large tents, holding three miners in two tents and the geologist in the third. They arranged in a semicircle, with a dimming campfire in the center of the circle. The tents opened to the campfire, about twenty paces.

In the center of the camp, Brave Eagle erected a cross with the tree branches bound by cloth. He placed the antelope's head atop the cross, with legs on either side, so it resembled a sort of antelope scarecrow. He soaked the cloth in kerosene, lit it afire and sprinted to higher ground.

From a higher perch, he shot three flaming arrows, one into each tent and he shouted with all his lungpower, a Lakota howl. The men frantically attempted to put out the flames with water.

Brave Eagle crept away to a small cave on the trail, and slept the rest of the night, awaking before sunrise. The miners slept in the open, their tents destroyed. Whether they remained or not was up to them. He considered how to torment the men further, terrorize them into leaving, but he went on his way. He gathered his blankets and mounted his chestnut mare to venture back to Rapid City.

As he descended a hill only a mile from his home, he encountered a dozen buffalo and in their midst, a pure white one. A white buffalo! Throughout his life he heard mention of an albino roaming the plains, said to possess mystical powers.

He edged closer to the pack and dismounted, stealthily creeping close to the grazing herd. As he approached, the herd trotted away a dozen yards, except for the white buffalo, that turned to consider the intruder.

Brave Eagle stood in front of the buffalo. Its pinkish eyes glared right at him as he extended his hand and placed it on her nose. She snorted at his touch and a mist of breath wet his palm.

"We are one, white buffalo," Brave Eagle spoke. He pet the buffalo's forehead and it grunted. As he stepped backwards-away form the buffalo, making sure it did not charge him, the buffalo turned and moved towards the rest of the herd, where it seemed to say, "Who is that man?"

"I am not crazy, white one," Brave Eagle said, reading its thoughts.

The sight of the white buffalo inspired Brave Eagle. And as he set off in the direction of home, he felt a sense of serenity. Then, he turned a blind corner in the hill and from behind a bush, a cougar leapt and the force of its 300 lithe pounds knocked him from his horse. The cat tumbled down the hill, rebounded and let out a terrifying shriek, barred its teeth and crept up the hill back towards Brave Eagle, who sprawled on the ground, his leg twisted from the fall. The horse galloped away in fear.

Brave Eagle stood one-legged, unable to bear weight on his right leg and unsheathed his knife. He crouched low, knowing the cat would spring, no running from this one.

The cougar crawled, its body coiled in preparation for its jump. Brave Eagle's shoulder throbbed with pain from the cougar's claws and his knee ached. He edged to his right and reached for a handful of dirt. As the cat moved another step on the verge of attack, Brave Eagle tossed the dirt in its face and it closed its eyes for a second, pulled its head back and as Brave Eagle reached for more dirt and jumped.

He thrust his knife upward as the full weight of the cat landed upon him, and plunged it deep into its neck as it landed on him and he twisted the blade across the throat as it gasped and gargled blood in his face. He faced the teeth of the lion as its neck reared back and eyes glazed over in death. The body of the lion lay on top of Brave Eagle and he pushed it aside. For minutes he lay on the ground, facing the sky, assessing the damage to his body. A huge gash on his forehead from the cougar's teeth bled into his eyes. He lost consciousness.

He was out for about ten minutes, but when he awoke, his face wet. An April snow came down hard. He staggered to his feet but the pain in his knee was excruciating as he stepped with his right foot.

A wagon approached and he struggled to a perch behind the bushes. A mule-drawn wagon with four miners clopped noisily. They stopped at the dead cougar and got out.

"Holy! Somebody slit the throat."

"Indians. They're out here. Get your rifles ready."

The men scanned the area and carefully climbed back into the wagon.

"We shoulda never come here, Bob."

"I told you, but no. You had to come and strike it rich. I am not sticking around to get my own throat slit. First day and they burn the tents down. One more night and they scalp us."

"This snow is gonna make it hard to get back. Come on, let's go!"

After the wagon passed, Brave Eagle emerged and assessed the situation. His blanket had fallen off the horse, and his bow and a quiver of arrows. He cut a strip of cloth from his shirt, dabbed the blood from his forehead and wrapped around his head. He searched the woods off the road until he found a sturdy stick for a walking cane. His knee throbbed with pain at every step, but he had to move.

He made slow progress, having to stop to take deep breaths every few steps when sharp pain halted him. The road turned a corner and began a descent that evened out to flat land, but as Brave Eagle turned the corner, the snow turned into a white out in horizontal sheets, hurting his face. He pulled the blanket over his head for protection. He turned his back to the rushing snow and walked back I the other direction, remembering a small inlet off the trail that provided a temporary oasis, and he huddled as the wind whipped the snow furiously.

The storm continued for more than two hours and by the time it subsided, two feet of snow had accumulated. Sundown approached, and with six to eight miles to Rapid City, he was in for a night. He found some degree of comfort in his little cave, and rather than test his ability to forge through the snow in the dark, he closed his eyes.

The morning after the snowfall, Onashola hurriedly prepared Betty Pettigrew's sleigh and two horses. Maka and Wishiwu fetched Sheriff Jameson, who arrived on horseback with two volunteers.

"What was his destination?" Jameson asked.

"He went to the mines in the hills."

"Hmm. I expect he's going to McEver's mines. It's going to be slow. We'll let the sleigh lead to carve a path for us. Our horses will get less tired."

Maka and Wishiwu boarded the sleigh next to their mother. It was a clear, sunny, morning, about 40 degrees.

"Please God, don't let anything happen to him!" Wishiwu prayed.

"I'm sure he's all right. Don't worry," Onashola reassured, trying to hide her own concern. "A little April snow can't stop him."

"Something may have happened with the miners."

"We'll find him."

Two hours later, in late morning, a rifle blast interrupted the silence and shortly after, they came upon the miners, their carriage stuck in a rut.

"Damn mules can't pull us out!" Four miners, filthy from dirt, shivering pleaded. "One of our men needs help!"

Sheriff Jameson looked inside the carriage and beheld a shaking pale miner.

"Uh, all right. He has to get back. Murray, let's get this man on your horse and bring him to the doctor. We're in search for a lost man. Anyone else on the trail?"

"No one."

"Why did you shoot?"

"We wanted to attract attention. We've been out here all night. I was about to start back on one of the mules and leave old Gant behind."

"Why did you leave the mine?"

"Indians. They set our tents on fire. I don't want to stay here and get scalped. So we left."

Onashola leaned in to Maka and whispered. "Brave Eagle."

"And where did you come from?"

"Follow our tracks. Into the hills about ten miles." the miner pointed back at the Black Hills. "It's the first canyon and go up the switchbacks. But be careful. But...." he stared at Onashola. "She's an Indian, right?"

She nodded.

He shrugged. "They didn't pay me for this. We're all from California and going back where we belong."

"We're off to find a man," Jameson instructed. "I suggest you unhook your mules and follow the sleigh tracks to Rapid City."

"Can't you help us pull the wagon out?"

"We must find the man. We can help later."

Leaving one of the volunteers behind to take the sick man to Rapid City, the entourage trudged back towards the hills.

Brave Eagle awoke to the sound of a rifle shot in the distance. He stirred and emerged from the small cave. It was morning and he never slept past dawn. The first step he took out of the cave served as a reminder - his knee was damaged. The throbbing pain was gone, but walking proved possible only if he either dragged his leg or skipped the right leg. It was easier to do skip. Then, the snow. It would take a while. He estimated he was five miles from home. Normally, he could walk in ninety minutes. But with skipping and the snow, he guessed he would make home in mid-afternoon.

Onashola was bound to be looking for him. He'd mentioned to her that he was headed up the path by Box elder Creek so if she penetrated the snow, she'd probably find him.

Brave Eagle wore shin-covering boots, but on this day, he appreciated them more than ever. Still, snow seeped inside the boots as he walked. It was warm by South Dakota standards for April, around 40 degrees and that would loosen he snow a bit.

Covered by a brown woolen blanket, he marched on, left, skip, left, skip, pause, bolstered by the stick.

He could make it. This was but one small journey among the many roads he traversed in his sixty plus years. Sweat dripped inside his clothes as he trudged on. He followed the tracks of the miner's wagon. Every ten minutes or so, he sat on the ground and collect his strength.

As noon approached, the sleigh approached and Onashola, Maka and Wishiwu vaulted from the sleigh when they reached him.

"Oh, you're dripping wet! What happened?" Onashola wept she embraced him and both Maka and Wishiwu put their arms around him.

"Chessie fell on me. I hurt my leg! A sprain. I'll be all right. Everything all right at home?"

"Yes. Bobby stayed with Betty. A group of miners said they were attacked by Indians."

"I put a scare into them."

"What did you do?"

"Lit their tents on fire, that's all."

"A dozen more arrived last night. They're going to keep coming."

Brave Eagle sighed. "Like Sitting Bull warned."

Jenkins eased into the younger McEver's office. "Uh, hate to disturb you..."

One of his women sat atop his lap, facing him and she turned and pulled her top to cover her exposed breasts.

"Don't you knock?"

"Some of the miners returned a carriage and left because they were attacked by Indians."

"Attacked way up there? Go on, get out of here," James McEver shoved the woman off his lap and she rushed out of the room.

"They said all their tents were set on fire and there was a lot of eerie Indian calls that scared them, so they left."

"I got twelve more to go out as the snow melts. We'll give them more rifles. But it's not like Indians to go all the way. Nobody lives there."

"Had to be Brave eagle's doing."

"The one that killed my uncle?"

"That's the one."

"I'll get rid of him by myself. Can't expect to count on anyone else."

"You ever killed anyone?"

'None of your business."

"He has a wife and children."

"Didn't stop my uncle from taking them. They are trouble, and multiply like rabbits. I won't get him by his house. I can in Rapid City. Does he go into town?"

"I've seen him."

"Where?"

"Everybody goes to the dry goods store."

"So that's where we will go, too."

"In the town?"

"No. What kind of question is that? I'm not getting into any shoot out. I know a way."

The next Saturday morning, James McEver stationed himself in the third floor hotel room facing the street. The hotel was next door to the dry goods store, and he learned it was Brave Eagle and Onashola's custom to shop as soon as the store opened at 9 am on Saturday. Jenkins knocked on the hotel door.

James opened the door slightly, "IS he there?"

"With Onashola and a little boy."

"How long does he usually take?"

"Thirty minutes."

"Fine, I'll wait."

He sat on a wooden chair looking out the window, thirty feet above the street with clear sight line. On the other side of the street, Brave Eagle's horse carriage was parked.

Inside the dry goods store, Brave Eagle and Onashola gathered a sack full of groceries, and obliged Bobby with a bag of candy. Brave Eagle limped still, but carried a bag of groceries in each arm, while Onashola held Bobby's hand and a bag of groceries with the other.

They were in the center of the street when the rifle blast rang out and the bullet passed through his buckskin coat under his armpit and he hit the ground. Bobby screamed and Onashola picked him up and ran for the protection of the carriage.

Brave Eagle lay on the ground, rolled over and another shot missed as the bullet hit the dirt inches form his head. He withdrew his pistol and saw the shooter take aim in the window of the hotel. Brave Eagle aimed and shot.

The shooter slumped out of the window and fell to the street.

Brave Eagle walked over to the man, looking around to make sure there was not a second gunman and turned him over.

"Who is he?" Onashola and Bobby stood over the dead man.

"Never saw him before." Brave Eagle lifted his jacket to reveal the gaping hole in his jacket. "Not a very good shot, thank God."

Sheriff Jameson ran out of the jailhouse and spectators gathered around the dead man.

"Anyone know this man?"

"I know him. "Jenkins stood over the body. "He's James McEver."

"What was he McEver's son?"

"Nephew."

"How many McEvers are there?"

"James has a father and a brother."

"So you better tell them to leave Rapid City alone. And what are you doing back here again?"

"I was hired to run his businesses. Guess that's over now."

"You bet. I'll get the undertaker. You come with me."

Brave Eagle returned to pick up his groceries scattered in the road, as Onashola placed Bobby in the carriage.

"Will this ever stop?" she said as Brave Eagle boarded.

He shrugged. "They're like buzzing mosquitoes. You keep swatting them away but they come back to taste your blood," he showed her the hole in his jacket.

That night, the Heard family and Sheriff Jameson were dinner guests at Betty Pettigrew's house. The four adults sat on rockers on the front porch. It was a pleasant early evening before sunset and Maka, Wishiwu and Bobby played catch with baseball mitts in the road in front of the house.

"How does it feel, sitting here, after being attacked by a mountain lion, buried in the snow and getting shot at all within a few days?" Jameson shook his head. "It's like you are invincible. God keep sending all these obstacles at you, one right after the other. You're either the unluckiest or the luckiest man alive."

"Let's not forget Little Big Horn and all those battles he fought in," Betty added.

"What Onashola went through, was worse."

"My family tried to talk me out of living in South Dakota," Betty said, "Excuse me while I check on the pie, it takes a certain character to thrive here."

"We're not leaving," Onashola said. "There is a reason we are here and I am watching them now."

"And they escaped the bad men and survived the San Francisco earthquake," Sheriff Jameson added. "They are just like their parents."

"We could move to Colorado or Arizona or Utah. There is a McEver in every town, in every city. I searched for tranquility and I have it at this moment. This is what I lived for and I will fight to the death to keep it. "

"Funny you should say that, because my next question to you is 'Are we going to stay here in South Dakota?"

"You know the answer."

"I do. I needn't have asked. After going through all this, this land is either driving to drive us away or asking us whether we have the strength to stay."

Betty excused herself to enter the house and Maka, Wishiwu and Bobby approached. Maka pounded the ball in her mitt.

"What are you all talking about, moving?"

"We're talking about why we stay here," Onashola said.

"I'd say we move to Colorado," Maka replied. "I liked it."

"Me, too," her sister added.

"Soon, you'll make the choice. You're almost a woman now and experienced more than some do in their entire lifetimes."

"We won't leave without our parents."

"Then you better get used to South Dakota."

"It's flat here."

"The Black Hills aren't flat."

"The last of the McEvers? I don't want to be at war all the time."

Sheriff Jameson joined in, "Might be some more in California. But the miners are all going to leave now. Without anyone to run their businesses, I doubt we'll see them again."

Brave Eagle shifted in his chair and a tweak in the knee caused him to grimace. Maka asked, "How is the knee?"

"I think I won't be challenging you in one mile races any more. Doesn't hurt unless I move it a certain way."

Maka, Wishiwu and Bobby sat on the porch steps, looking at the road. The conversation stopped dead for several minutes, and the sound of crickets magnified.

Bobby said, "What are we looking at?"

"The Ghost of Christmas future," Maka laughed.

And what they saw. The woods across the dirt road, with narrow walking paths and even narrower deer trails. Beyond the woods, the flat lands that led to the Black Hills.

Brave Eagle grasped Onashola's hand. "Home," he said.

Onashola smiled and squeezed his hand. "Is in front of our eyes."

About the Author

Scott Thomas Young is a professor of management and the author of three books on management.

Young lives in Wilmette, Illinois, with his wife and daughters.

Black Hills Gold is his first novel.

www.ingramcontent.com/pod-product-compliance
Lightning Source LLC
Chambersburg PA
CBHW072353190626
46811CB00019B/772